“Birchfie[illegible] Em[illegible] Said the Operator.

“Yes . . . hello. I’d like to report a . . . there’s a girl in trouble,” Philip Joyce stammered into the receiver. He wished fervently that he’d never come out tonight, never left the fraternity house.

The operator punched a button on the console in front of her and automatically activated the tape recorder.

“Sir,” she said crisply, “may I have your name, please.”

Philip shook his head and grimaced. “Listen,” he reiterated more urgently, “there’s a girl in trouble. It’s the Mill. It’s a bar on Mill Road.”

“Sir, I’m sorry,” the operator said calmly, “I must have your . . .”

A horn blared. Jerking his head in its direction, Philip caught sight of the girl, staggering down the yellow centerline of the highway. Cars swerved to avoid hitting her.

Philip gripped the phone tightly. “She’s hurt. There’s an assault going on . . . a rape, Okay? Three, four . . . I don’t know . . . there’s a crowd.”

“Sir, if you’d please—”

Philip slammed down the receiver and raced out of the booth and onto the road, toward the girl. . . .

THE ACCUSED

A NOVEL BY DEBORAH CHIEL
BASED ON THE SCREENPLAY
WRITTEN BY TOM TOPOR

Futura

A Futura Book

First published in Great Britain in 1988
by Futura Publications,
a Division of Macdonald & Co (Publishers) Ltd
London & Sydney, under exclusive licence from
Paramount Pictures Corporation

All characters in this publication are fictitious and any resemblance to real persons, living or dead, is purely coincidental.

ISBN 0 7088 4267 4

Reproduced, printed and bound in Great Britain by
Hazell Watson & Viney Limited
Member of BPCC plc
Aylesbury, Bucks, England

Futura Publications
A Division of
Macdonald & Co (Publishers) Ltd
Greater London House
Hampstead Road
London NW1 7QX
A member of Maxwell Pergamon Publishing Corporation plc

THE ACCUSED

CHAPTER ONE

The Mill was a friendly, raucous, slightly seedy bar, much like the many other bars that dotted the working-class neighborhoods of Portland. It was rather more dilapidated than some. The squat one-story building looked as if it might sink into the ground any day now with a great, clattering sigh, and the flickering blue neon sign proclaiming the Mill's existence was just barely visible from the road.

But neither the disreputable exterior nor the shabby, smoky interior discouraged the regulars, who stopped by every day after work to grab a few beers and hang out with their buddies. It was the kind of place where the men usually outnumbered the women and the menu was strictly peanuts and booze.

This dreary Saturday night in April was no exception. Rain had been falling steadily since Friday morning—a relentless spring rain that soaked through raincoats and rubber boots and left behind deep, muddy puddles. But the cold, soggy weather hadn't dampened spirits, and the garbage-strewn parking lot in front of the Mill was crowded with American-made cars and battered pickup trucks. The muffled roar of the traffic passing on the nearby highway was drowned out by the loud laughter and pounding jukebox music that burst out of the bar each time the front door swung open and shut.

The bar door swung open again, and a sudden, sharp noise pierced the night air. A thin young woman stood silhouetted in the doorway, gulping for breath. Tears streamed down her cheeks, and her blond hair flew crazily about her face and shoulders. She shivered as she tugged at her pink sweatshirt, pulling it down as far as she could to cover herself. Below her waist she was naked.

The young woman whimpered as if she were in pain and took one uncertain step forward. The woman darted a wild-eyed glance behind her into the bar.

"No!" she shrieked, her voice rising shrilly. "No! No! No!"

Then, like a wounded animal bent on escaping its pursuers, she bolted across the parking lot. Oblivious to the cold water splashing her bare legs and ankles, she dashed blindly in the direction of the highway.

Philip Joyce peered anxiously through the rain-streaked glass of the phone booth, located about a hundred feet down from the Mill parking lot. An athletically built, good-looking young man, he was panting as if he had just set a record for the hundred-yard dash.

Despite the chill, damp air, Philip was sweating heavily beneath his light windbreaker as he waited impatiently for his call to work its way through the telephone circuits. A couple of seconds later, the connection was made. The phone at the other end finally began to ring.

"Birchfield County Sheriff, Emergency," said the operator.

"Yes . . . hello. I'd like to report a . . . there's a girl in trouble," Philip stammered into the receiver.

The operator swung into her standard operating procedure and automatically activated the tape recorder.

"Sir," she said crisply, "may I have your name, please?"

Philip shook his head and grimaced. "Listen," he reiterated more urgently, "there's a girl in trouble. It's the Mill. It's a bar on Mill Road."

"Sir, I'm sorry," the operator said calmly. "I must have your . . ."

Philip squinted through the glare of the street lamp above the phone booth, searching the night for signs of life.

A horn blared.

Jerking his head in its direction, he caught sight of the girl, staggering down the yellow centerline of the highway.

More horns blared. A couple of drivers yelled angrily and swerved to avoid hitting the girl.

Philip gripped the phone tightly. "She's hurt. There's an assault going on . . . a rape, okay? Three, four . . . I don't know . . . there's a crowd."

"Sir, if you'd please—"

Philip slammed down the receiver and raced out of the booth and onto the road, toward the girl. Was she crazy? She would get herself killed if she didn't get the hell out of the traffic.

But she seemed oblivious to the danger as she continued to weave along the road, spotlighted by the oncoming headlights of cars and trucks.

Philip had covered more than half the distance when a set of brakes squealed loudly. A pickup truck screeched to a halt just short of the girl and backed up a few feet to retrieve her.

Deputy District Attorney Katheryn Murphy made love the way she argued a case in court—with a lot of carefully controlled passion and one eye always focused on her audience to gauge her effect.

At twenty-eight, Katheryn was more than merely pretty. She was built big and long-limbed, with honey-blond hair and blue eyes. Her current lover, David, was also a lawyer.

On this Saturday evening, they had settled into Katheryn's bed and were folded in each other's arms when they were interupted by the phone ringing. Taking a deep breath, Katheryn picked up the receiver. "Hello?"

"Hi, Katheryn. It's Dunc."

Ed Duncan was a dependable, hardworking detective who made up in doggedness what he lacked in imagination. He had been her police contact on more cases than she could count. But she wasn't on call tonight, and she was annoyed by his interruption. Glancing at the clock radio on her night table, she saw that it was almost one o'clock.

"I'm not catching tonight, Dunc," she said brusquely, signaling David that she would just be a minute.

Dunc sounded apologetic. "Yes you are. Vivian's sick. Meet me at Central Receiving as soon as you can. And bring a set of clothes."

There was no point in arguing. Besides, Dunc was a good pal. "Okay," she sighed. "See you."

She turned to David and shrugged wordlessly, not bothering to explain. She knew he understood. He had done his time in the D.A.'s office some years back.

David brushed back the strands of blond hair that had fallen across her face, kissed her, and said, "Work?"

Katheryn smiled apologetically and jumped out of bed, stooping to retrieve her underwear.

"Work," she said.

Of all the bad luck.

CHAPTER TWO

"TURN THIS WAY, HONEY. THAT'S GOOD. JUST raise your chin a tad. Good, now the other side . . ."

The orderly hated this part of her job, having to take Polaroid shots of the girls. And some of them seemed so pathetic, like this poor little thing with the ugly bruises all over her face. She knew the pictures were needed as evidence, but still, it always seemed so heartless and cruel, making them turn this way and that, as though they were posing for some grim version of a wedding album.

This one hardly seemed to be paying attention, sitting there so quietly on the examining table, looking as if she might drown in the oversize hospital gown. The orderly smiled encouragingly at the girl—Sarah, her name was—and looked over at the nurse to see whether she needed anything else.

Sometimes, depending on what they found during the physical exam, the nurses asked for a couple more photos. There was a whole routine to be followed, to make it easier on the girls. The idea was to act nice and calm, so as not to make them feel as if *they* were the criminals.

The poor things, lots of them couldn't stop crying—though some of them were like this Sarah, just sitting there so quietly, while Deborah, the nurse, went through the list of questions.

"What kind of contraceptive do you normally use?" Deborah was asking her.

"IUD," Sarah said, almost in a whisper.

"When was your last period?"

"April second. Bad cramps."

"What's your usual cycle?"

"Twenty-six, twenty-seven days." Sarah's head was aching as if it had taken a direct hit from a sledgehammer. She wished the nurse would speed it up so she could take a shower and get out of there.

"Aren't you going to examine me?" she said plaintively.

"I need some more history first," Deborah explained, pointing to her clipboard. "Before the incident, when was your last intercourse?"

"A while."

"Can you be more specific?"

"Couple of days . . . a week."

"You're sure?"

"Yeah," Sarah said softly.

"Have you ever had a venereal disease?" asked Deborah.

Sarah shook her head and folded her arms tightly

across her chest, as if to protect herself from the barrage of questions.

A neatly dressed woman poked her head in the doorway, nodded at Deborah, and came inside.

"How do you do, Sarah?" she said, touching her briefly on the arm. "I'm Carol Honeycutt from the Rape Center. Is there anyone you'd like me to call?"

Sarah stared fiercely at the gray and black tiles on the examining-room floor. She shook her head no.

Carol Honeycutt stared at Sarah for a moment, then picked up the photographs and looked carefully at each one in turn. Then she moved closer to Sarah and said, "I'm here to help, so let me know if I can do anything, okay?"

Sarah scowled. There was nothing Carol Honeycutt or anyone else could do except get her out of there. She wanted to lock herself in the bathroom and take a very long steaming-hot bath. And get loaded enough to block out the memory of what those bastards had done to her.

The Mill was quieter than it had been all night. The TV was turned down low, and the jukebox was playing a doleful western song about lost love. Most of the guys had ordered one for the road, settled up with the bartender, and left for home. Only a few of the diehards remained—Danny Maquette and Kurt Wolpe were half-asleep at the bar; Arthur Polito was bending the bartender's ear with some cockeyed money-making scheme.

Jesse had heard them all before. But Arthur was an okay guy, and the way Jesse saw it, being a good listener came with the territory. He poured Arthur another scotch, checked to see whether everyone else was okay, and fished around in the bucket beneath the counter for a wet rag.

He was looking forward to closing up. It had been a long night, what with the guys getting a little crazy before and having their fun in the back room. He could have lived without all the commotion—it hadn't done a thing for business.

The door opened. The cop on the beat, walked in. He shook a spray of water off his cap and strolled over to the bar.

"Nightcap?" asked Jesse.

The cop shook his head. "You have any trouble here tonight?" he asked.

Jesse sopped up a melting ice cube someone had spilled on the drink-stained wooden bar. "The usual," he shrugged. "Saturday night . . . nothin' special."

"We got a call about a rape," said Joe, taking a quick look around.

"Rape? You're puttin' me on." Jesse chuckled mirthlessly. "These guys can't get it up. They're boozers." He leaned closer to the cop and lowered his voice slightly. "We had a couple of kids from the college . . . real 'party animals,' y'know what I'm sayin'?"

Joe nodded and winked. College kids, spoiled little bastards who couldn't hold their booze. He wished they'd stay the hell out of his neighborhood.

"Yeah, right," he said, nodding again. "Thanks."

Jesse smiled. "Hey, no problem."

* * *

"Try to relax," Deborah told Sarah.

Sarah clenched her fists and gasped as the cold metal of the speculum slid inside her. Flat on her back, her legs positioned in the stirrups on either side of the examining table, she closed her eyes and tried to think about summer at the lake and suntanning in the hot midday sun.

"You're tensing. Hold on," said Deborah.

Opening her eyes, she flinched as Deborah deftly removed the first speculum and inserted a second. "Easy . . . easy . . . okay."

"The smear's on the house," Deborah quipped as she reached for the Pap stick.

Sarah rewarded her with a wan smile.

CHAPTER THREE

"NOW," SAID DEBORAH, A SYRINGE IN HER RIGHT hand, "a little blood."

Sarah flinched but didn't make a sound. She was so tired . . .

Deborah picked up a fine-toothed comb and glanced at Carol, who was standing next to the examining table.

"She's combing for hairs," Carol explained. "Not yours. Theirs."

"Good," Deborah said. "You can sit up now. We're almost done. Put your hands out, just for a second or two."

She held up a pointed orange stick. "Their skin," she said, as she began to gently scrape beneath Sarah's fingernails.

Sarah stared at the bruises on her arms and legs. They must have done quite a job on her face, too. Her lips felt puffy and swollen, and the bruise on her forehead was aching something awful. What a sight she must be!

She was about to ask the nurse for a mirror when there was a knock on the door. She felt like saying, hey, she really wasn't in the mood for visitors.

But Carol was already at the door. She said, "Hi, come on in," like this was some damn cocktail party or something. And now she was making introductions, saying, "Sarah, this is Katheryn Murphy. She'll be the deputy district attorney for your case."

"Hi, Sarah," Katheryn said. She put down a shopping bag that contained a dress and a change of underwear for Sarah.

"Hi," Sarah said, wishing they would all take a hike.

"Are you allergic to penicillin?" asked Deborah.

"In case any of them had anything," Carol said quickly.

Sarah shook her head and turned over onto her stomach so Deborah could give her the shot.

Her eyes met Katheryn Murphy's. The deputy D.A. was staring at her as if she were trying to place her, as if they had met before.

They hadn't, of course. But Sarah Tobias appeared to be about her own age, and Katheryn had known plenty of girls just like her in high school. Girls who didn't have the self-discipline or the willpower to make something of themselves, something more than where they came from. They were born victims. They spent their whole lives making messes, then trying to get other, more responsible people to clean up after them.

Personally, Katheryn had nothing but contempt for

these weak sisters. But professionally, she was bound to maintain a careful neutrality in order to represent and defend their interests when necessary. Still, she had a strong gut feeling that whatever Sarah's story was, it wouldn't hold water. Probably she had gotten exactly what she deserved.

She watched Sarah wince with pain as the injection found its mark.

That done, Deborah said, "Okay, you can take a shower now . . . and a douche."

Carol helped her off the table. "The ladies' room is down the hall," she said. "The shower's on your left, as you go in."

Sarah nodded and limped toward the door. Then suddenly she remembered that except for her sweatshirt, which was sopping wet, she had nothing to wear.

Katheryn seemed to read her mind. "I hope you don't mind gray," she said, offering Sarah the shopping bag.

As long as the clothes were dry and clean, she didn't give a damn what color they were. Halfway out the door, she thought of something else.

"Have you got any mouthwash?" she asked in a small, tired voice, feeling unaccountably ashamed.

Deborah handed her a bottle, and Sarah left the room.

Now that she had been taken care of, the three women turned their attention to the paperwork. While Deborah and Carol were busy finishing their reports, Katheryn read through Sarah's chart, taking notes as she went along.

One item didn't surprise her at all. "Lot of alcohol," she commented aloud.

"Legally drunk," Carol said, not looking up.

"Grass, too. Anything else?"

Something in her voice caught Carol's attention. "What difference does it make? She was raped by three men."

"Carol," Katheryn said coolly, "I'm not a rape counselor. I'm a prosecutor, and I have to make a rape case."

Carol gave Katheryn a hard, appraising stare. "Then go prosecute," she said, wanting to add, *It's the men who deserve to be prosecuted, not the victim.*

Katheryn handed the clipboard back to Deborah. "Tell her I'll wait in the supervisor's office."

She left the room without bothering to say goodbye.

"The music stopped," Sarah said. "I heard somebody crying, and it was me. Catchy, huh?"

She hummed a tune that sounded like any one of a thousand melancholy country ballads.

Outside in the hospital corridor, Dunc stood listening for a moment before joining Sarah and Katheryn in the sparsely furnished office.

She welcomed him with a smile and introduced him. "Sarah, this is Detective Duncan."

Dunc stuck out his hand. "Dunc," he said casually. "How you doin'?"

He shot Katheryn a look to indicate that she should go ahead and ask the questions. He would just listen for a while. Katheryn had a way sometimes of digging out information that other people missed. Besides, right now the girl was more likely to talk to another woman than to a male cop.

"Would you recognize any of the men?" Katheryn asked.

Sarah didn't have to think twice about that one. Damn straight she would. She nodded. Absolutely.

Katheryn checked her watch and said, "The Mill is still open. We'd like you to go over there with us and see if you can make a positive ID."

"Oh shit," Sarah swore softly. The Mill was the last place on earth she ever wanted to set foot in again.

"We'll be right there with you," Dunc assured her.

Big deal. The idea of having to walk in there again tonight, of seeing those bastards, maybe even having to talk to them . . .

"Sarah," Katheryn said calmly, "if you want to get them, I need your help every step of the way."

Yeah, that was what she wanted—to get them. Okay, she nodded. Yes.

"I'll pick up a warrant and meet you there," Katheryn told Dunc.

The license plate on the beat-up canary-yellow Camaro was personalized: SXY SADI.

Katheryn pulled in next to the Camaro. She didn't need two guesses to figure out who the car belonged to. Dunc was right behind her with Sarah, and a patrol car brought up the rear.

The rain had stopped, but the air was damp and chilly. A thick curtain of cigarette smoke shrouded the inside of the Mill, but at least it was warm. The bartender was wiping down the tables, while two men were watching television at the bar. A third was passed out cold in one of the booths.

Sarah kept her eyes to herself and clung to Dunc's arm as if he were her life preserver in the middle of a shark-infested ocean. When Arthur Polito glanced her way, she gulped and squeezed Dunc hard enough to make him wince.

"Okay," Katheryn said quietly, her back to the bar. "Can you identify any of your attackers? Don't point. Don't turn your head. And don't tell me. Tell Detective Duncan."

Sarah licked her lips nervously as she spoke. "To your left . . . the dark one in the plaid shirt and the one in the beige sweater."

Katheryn turned to Dunc and said under her breath, "Did you hear her?"

He nodded almost imperceptibly.

"Sarah," Katheryn said quietly, "wait in my car for me." She motioned to one of the cops to take Sarah outside.

Then she turned on her official voice. "I'm Katheryn Murphy, deputy district attorney in Birchfield County. We have a report of a felony—"

"What felony?" Jesse interrupted her.

". . . on these premises," Katheryn continued as if he hadn't said a word. She held up a piece of paper. "This is a search warrant signed by Judge Cutler, and this is Detective Duncan. He's in charge of the investigation."

Dunc helped himself to a handful of peanuts from a bowl on the bar.

"You wanna turn off the TV so we can talk in peace?" he said amicably.

He smiled at Arthur Polito, as if he were noticing him for the first time. "Hey, Polito, how ya been? Didn't figure you'd be out for a couple of years."

Polito took a long, angry drag on his cigarette and scowled at the detective. Here he was, minding his own business, and already Duncan was trying to finger him. A guy couldn't even get himself a couple of drinks at the corner bar without someone looking to make trouble for him.

Sarah didn't bother to ask if she could smoke in Katheryn's car. She badly needed the cigarette, and if Katheryn didn't like it, tough luck. But she did roll down the window a couple of inches and was careful to blow the smoke outside. She didn't much like this lady lawyer, but she seemed to be stuck with her. And she wanted Katheryn Murphy on her side.

The inside of Katheryn's blue Taurus was spotlessly clean. No old newspapers on the back seat, no gum wrappers, not even a cigarette butt in the ashtray. Sarah was willing to bet that she kept her home the same way—nothing out of place, everything tidy and neat.

The car radio was on. Sarah listened for a while, quietly humming the song. Then she said, "The college one wasn't there. Kurt, Danny, and the college one. I don't know the others."

"What others?" Katheryn glanced at her, puzzled.

"The ones who yelled and clapped. Bob is the

college one . . . Bob Joiner. Did you go to college? Oh yeah." She remembered, embarrassed. "I forgot. You're a lawyer." She listened to a few bars of the next song, wanting to protest, *Hey, just because I asked a dumb question doesn't mean I'm stupid.* She'd been through a hell of a lot tonight. It was a miracle she could still put two sentences together.

"Who was yelling and clapping?"

"A whole bunch of them. They played pinball on the machine. My girlfriend Sally was there."

Katheryn couldn't get a handle on Sarah. The internal exam and the bruises all over her face and body attested to the fact that she had had a rough time. But here she sat, cool as an ice cube. And who were these "others" she had mentioned?

Sarah finished her cigarette and carefully flicked it out the window. "It's right up there," she said, pointing. "The trailer. Maybe you better stop here. He's asleep. See, he gets stoned and takes the phone off the hook."

But even after Katheryn had pulled over and shifted the car into neutral, Sarah didn't make a move to get out.

"Are you okay?" Katheryn asked.

Sarah shook her head. "I don't know. My eyes hurt. Are you married?"

"No." Katheryn wasn't eager to pursue this conversation. She was tired and ready to be on her way. "Are you?"

"No. My mother's been married for thirty years, but he left when I was born." She shifted in her seat and looked at Katheryn. "Are you into astrology?"

"No, I'm not."

"Too bad. I could do your chart. When were you born?"

"Nineteen fifty-nine," Katheryn said reluctantly.

"Boy, I sure hope I can wake him." Sarah stared absently through the windshield into the dark, starless night.

"Do you want me to go in with you?" Katheryn suggested, surprised to hear herself making the offer and hoping Sarah wouldn't take her up on it.

Sarah hesitated, then shook her head no and quickly opened the door.

"Wait," said Katheryn. She searched in her purse until she found a business card. "Here's my card. If you need anything, call, okay?"

The overhead light threw distorted shadows across Sarah's face as she hesitated, already halfway out the door. She stared at the card, as if she were studying it for clues that would help her understand how she happened to be there.

"Where's my car?" she said suddenly, sounding panicked.

"A policeman will bring it back tomorrow. Camaro, right?"

Katheryn peered at Sarah, trying to make out whether she might be on the verge of falling apart.

With a quick, sharp nod, Sarah rearranged her face and said, "The keys fell out. They're probably on the floor." Her mouth smelling of mint-flavored mouthwash, she leaned close to Katheryn and asked, "Does my face look real bad?"

"No," Katheryn lied.

"He likes to touch my face . . ."

Then she bolted out of the car and hurried up the gravel road toward the trailer.

Katheryn watched her until she reached the top of the path. She felt an unexpected flash of sympathy for the other woman. *There but for the grace . . .*

But no, she assured herself, never, ever could such a thing have happened to her. *She* knew how to take care of herself and keep out of trouble. Her life had nothing to do with Sarah Tobias's.

She pulled out her notebook and jotted down a few quick lines. Then, finally, she shifted into drive and headed for home.

CHAPTER FOUR

ONCE EVERY COUPLE OF MONTHS, SARAH WOULD take a good look around her trailer and get fed up with the overflowing ashtrays, the empty beer cans, the unfinished astrology charts, the crumpled bags of stale Doritos and potato chips, the cardboard containers of Chinese food and rotting vegetables in her refrigerator. She would spring into action and spend a day throwing out all the garbage, cleaning the bathroom, dusting and sweeping and shaking out the rugs.

In between cleanups, she coexisted with the disorder, maintaining a clutter-free zone on the bed she shared with her dog Sadie and, for the time being, Larry.

It had been a while now since her last blitz, and the place looked it. But this afternoon she was oblivious to the mess. She was feeling exhausted and bruised, with an achiness that went bone-deep, as if she were coming down with the flu. She knew she could get rid of flu symptoms by spending a couple of days in bed and swallowing aspirins. But she would need a lot more than bed rest to recover from what was ailing her.

Larry had tried to put his arms around her, but she was still so mad at him that she had pushed him away and locked herself in the bathroom so she could cry in peace.

She soaked in a bubble bath for a long time. When she came out, she threw on Katheryn's dress, which she had dropped on the floor the night before. Without a word to Larry, who was cooking eggs, she plopped down on the bed and plugged herself into her Walkman. As usual, Sadie immediately cuddled up next to her, wagging her tail and begging for attention.

Sarah's eyes focused blankly on the astrology poster on the opposite wall. She absentmindedly petted Sadie as the music filled the space between her ears.

Larry brought her a cup of coffee and tugged at one of her earphones.

"I wish I knew what to say," he mumbled, awkwardly patting her hair.

Sarah stared at him sullenly, immersed in the music.

"You wanna take a drive?"

"A drive?"

"Get some air. Cool out."

Sarah shook her head scornfully, then retreated again behind the earphones.

"Then I'll be back in a few minutes, okay?"

Without waiting to hear her answer, he stood up quickly and walked away.

Sarah watched him disappear out the door. *Bastard!* she wanted to call after him. *Goddamn bastard . . . you don't even care!*

Nobody cared.

Not Larry. Not that nurse last night with all her questions. Not the rape center lady who kept telling her to "come by anytime and talk to us." To say what? That a bunch of drunks—animals, they were—had used her to get their rocks off?

And that stuck-up chick from the D.A.'s office, she sure didn't care. She'd probably had it easy all her life, probably had no idea what it meant to have to take care of yourself, to have to fight to get a fair break once in a while.

Thanks for nothing, Katheryn Murphy.

Bored with the lack of attention, Sadie shook herself awake, jumped off the bed, and wandered away toward the kitchen.

Great. Even her goddamn dog didn't care.

Sarah lit a cigarette, fidgeted with her Walkman, then picked up the phone.

Her mother answered on the third ring.

"Hi," said Sarah, trying to sound upbeat. "No, no special reason, I just figured I'd say hello . . ." She reached for the ashtray. "Yeah, still waitressing. How's Amos? . . . Already? . . . I wasn't making fun of you, Ma." She protested halfheartedly. "No, I don't want any money. What I was thinkin', I was kinda thinkin' about comin' down there for a few days . . ."

She shook another cigarette out of the pack and lit it off the tip of the last one. "No, I'm not in any trouble, I just figured . . . Where? . . . Mexico? I like Mexico

. . . Oh, yeah, sure, I understand. What's his name? . . . Hey, Ma, you have a great time, okay? . . . Sadie's fine . . . Yeah, real soon. 'Bye."

Add one more name to the list of people who didn't give a damn about Sarah Tobias.

Earning the badge of bona fide star at the D.A.'s office meant putting in the hours—evenings, Saturdays, sometimes even Sundays, when a case was hot. A D.A.'s personal life played second fiddle to the files on his or her desk.

When she sat around, drinking and gossiping with her colleagues, Katheryn did her share of griping. Dates? How and when was she supposed to meet men? Sure, her new apartment was great. Too bad it still looked as if she had just moved in because she never had time to go furniture shopping. Good thing she *liked* the minimalist look.

But the truth was she thrived under pressure. The hard work and the deadlines excited her. The cross-examinations and summations made her feel the way she sometimes did after great sex: powerful, in command, desirable.

Her single-mindedness was about to pay off.

She had paid her dues. Soon she would be reaping the benefits.

Although she had been up half the night with Sarah Tobias, she spent most of the day at the office, working on Sarah's case and catching up with the backlog. Now all she wanted was a quiet evening in front of the TV and to be in bed by eleven.

The phone was already ringing when she walked

through the door of her apartment. She thought, *David?* then remembered that he had tickets for the basketball game. Glaring at the phone, she dared herself not to answer it. But with an apprehensive sigh, she quickly switched on the light, dropped her briefcase and bag on the dining-room table, and reached for the phone in the kitchen.

"Hello?"

All she could hear at the other end was the sound of a woman sobbing. Then, "Kathy?"

A familiar wave of anxiety hit her as she recognized her sister's voice. A call from Connie was never good news. She got in touch only when she needed help.

"Connie," she said, trying to mask her uneasiness. "What's wrong?"

More sobs, then Connie said thickly, "Jay and I broke up. He wants me out of here . . . tomorrow."

"Oh no." Katheryn clucked sympathetically. She peered into the refrigerator. A lonely carton of orange juice sat on the top shelf. She hadn't shopped in days. Emptying what was left of the juice into a glass, she asked, "Did you call Mom? Maybe you should stay there for a couple of days."

"She's taking care of Bob's wife and kids," Connie told her.

"Again?" She stretched the phone cord into the dining room and pulled the Polaroid shots of Sarah Tobias out of her briefcase.

As if sensing her lack of attention, Connie got to the point of her call. "I'd like to stay with *you.*"

Katheryn made a face into the phone. "Connie, I'm not really set up for that," she said pleadingly.

Connie pressed, "You have a couch."

And you have a lot of nerve. "I have a better idea," Katheryn said quickly. "Let me help you rent your own place."

Spreading the Polaroids across the tabletop, she pretended not to hear her sister's loud, irritated sigh.

"Dammit," Connie snapped. "I'm not after a charity check. I just don't want to be by myself right now. I've been alone too much as it is."

"Connie," Katheryn shot back, "you haven't spent a night by yourself since you were sixteen years old."

She was instantly remorseful. Another old pattern. Connie's demands and irresponsibility would drive her to lash out. Then she would be consumed with guilt because Connie seemed so incapable of defending herself.

"I'm sorry," Katheryn stammered. "I was just kidding."

But the line had already gone dead.

"Shit," she muttered, hanging up the phone. She stared at the Polaroids for a few moments. Then she sighed heavily and turned off the light. Forget about dinner. Between the photos of Sarah and Connie's call, she had totally lost her appetite.

CHAPTER FIVE

THE NEXT STEP WAS TO TRACK DOWN AND ARREST the suspect Sarah had referred to as "the college one," Bob Joiner. Katheryn and Sarah waited in Katheryn's car, watching the entrance to Joiner's fraternity house.

Dunc was parked across the street, and another police car was parked behind Katheryn.

Puffing nervously on her cigarette, Sarah said, "I always figured I'd work as a waitress till I found something that really turned me on. I'm still looking. Did you always know what you wanted to do?"

"Not always, but pretty early," said Katheryn.

"That's great," Sarah said, wishing she could ask her how you knew something like that. "Hey, isn't it a lot of money to go to law school?"

Katheryn drummed her fingers on the steering wheel. "I worked," she said tersely.

"I went to school for a while, but it was such a hassle—"

Sarah stiffened as she spotted Bob Joiner and the boy he'd been with the other night coming out of the frat house with a couple of other kids. She grabbed Katheryn's arm, and Katheryn tooted her horn briefly to catch Dunc's attention. Sarah nodded and pointed to Bob.

It took only a moment for Dunc and the other two cops to jump out of their cars and cross the lawn. They formed a circle around Bob and his frat brothers, pushed Bob up against the hood of a car, and handcuffed his hands behind his back.

Sarah felt as if she were watching a movie in which she played a brief but starring role. Except that the movie wasn't about her. It was about a guy who thought he could get away with whatever he wanted, then acted stunned and surprised when he was caught.

Had he truly believed that nobody would find him out? Did he really think he had the right to rape her and not have to pay for it?

Katheryn stood before the bench, flanked by the defense attorneys for Danny Maquette, Kurt Wolpe, and Bob Joiner. Also present were the defendants' families and reporters from the local press.

It was easy to pick out Bob Joiner's father. He had thinning black hair and a prominent forehead, just like his son. And in his three-piece pin-striped suit, he was better dressed than anyone else in the courtroom, except for the two men seated in the back row.

They watched attentively and whispered between themselves as Katheryn and the defense attorneys differed heatedly about the amount of bail. Their arguments bounced back and forth like a tennis ball at a championship match.

Katheryn spoke first. "Your honor, we expect to indict for first-degree felony."

George Henley, Joiner's lawyer, jumped right in. "Your honor, my client has no prior record—"

"In a crime like this," Katheryn broke in, "there is a genuine risk of defendants' fleeing the jurisdiction."

The judge peered down at Sam Dalton, who was known for taking on—and winning—seemingly hopeless cases. "Your honor, my client has roots in the community," he said.

"I'd like Mr. Joiner released to his family without bail," Henley declared.

"I'd like the same, your honor," Dalton chimed in.

Henry Sklar, the third defense attorney, went on record with the same request.

"Your honor, this is a crime of violence," argued Katheryn, "and the victim has a legitimate concern for her safety."

The judge raised his hand to signal them all to silence. He took several minutes to flip through the papers filed earlier with the court, then looked over at the defendants, as if to assess for himself their reliability.

Finally, he said, "Ten thousand dollars, each."

The hollow thump of his gavel echoed through the courtroom. As he left the bench, a buzz of "Nice going . . . Congratulations" passed among the three defense attorneys.

On her way out, Katheryn caught Sam Dalton glancing at her with a sly, triumphant grin.

Smile now, she told him silently. *Because you won't be smiling for long.*

She turned her gaze to the back of the courtroom, to the two sets of eyes that had been watching her, and smiled at David and at Ted Millbank, the senior partner in David's law firm.

She had a message for them, too.

Don't worry, she mentally telegraphed across the room. *Occasionally I lose a battle, but I never lose the war.*

CHAPTER SIX

The restraurant where Katheryn had joined David and Ted Millbank for lunch was very elegant—the kind of place where the staff boasted captains as well as a host, waiters, and busboys. It was evident to all concerned that a mutual professional seduction was taking place.

Millbank had suggested that Katheryn order veal for her main course so that they could drink a red that he particularly recommended.

So much for getting any work done this afternoon, thought Katheryn, watching Millbank sniff the cork from the bottle he had chosen. He savored the bouquet, then slowly sipped the wine. At his nod of approval, the waiter filled first Katheryn's and then David's glass.

"This is a nice little red, isn't it?" said Millbank. Pleased with his selection, he got down to the real reason for the lunch. "I only hope you won't be bored when you join us, Ms. Murphy. The only criminal work we do is as a courtesy to our corporate clients. Usually it involves mundane things like insider trading or stock fraud."

"No more sex and violence, Katheryn," joked David.

Katheryn smiled. "Well, sex and violence are fun, but—"

"They don't lead anywhere?" Millbank finished her thought.

"Only to more sex and violence."

"Do you have many pending cases, Ms. Murphy?"

Anticipating this question, she had reviewed her files early that morning, before leaving for court. "The usual. A felony murder, an arson, a couple of armed robberies, the rape . . ."

Millbank lowered his voice. "A fascinating antitrust case was just brought to us."

"It's bound to go all the way to the Supreme Court," David chimed in.

"We think it's the kind of case you could do wonders with."

"I'm flattered."

"Are you committed to seeing all your cases through to their resolutions?" Millbank's tone perfectly conveyed the answer he expected of her.

David cleared his throat. "Ted is always more comfortable when—"

"When his lawyers handle a major case right from the start?"

Millbank smiled at her careful summation. "Precisely."

Katheryn smiled back. "I'm more comfortable that way myself."

She was having fun, aware that, for the moment, she had the advantage. She knew exactly what Millbank wanted to hear from her.

It puzzled her when people complained about getting nervous and fluffing interviews. She enjoyed the give-and-take, the mutual seduction that was inherent in the process. Now she demurely lowered her eyes and took a bite of her veal piccata.

The ball was in Millbank's court. But adroit negotiator that he was, he preferred to take his time before putting his offer on the table.

With a discreet gesture to David to keep quiet, he leaned forward and said, "Ms. Murphy, this is such a pleasant place, and it's such a pleasure to chat with you. Would you mind very much if we saved our discussion about . . . compensation . . . until I come back from Tokyo? I'm sure we'll have no difficulty reaching an agreement."

Katheryn smiled graciously. "I'm sure, too," she said.

Pleased with herself, she picked up the bottle of wine. Without bothering to ask whether they wanted more, she refilled both men's glasses, then her own. It was a gesture that was meant to signify. Ted Millbank nodded his thanks. He understood perfectly.

The atmosphere at the Dugout Restaurant was a far cry from the quiet graciousness of the Manor House. The Dugout offered overstuffed sandwiches, deluxe burgers, something that passed for steak, and ice cream desserts with fancy toppings and fanciful names.

Sarah had been working there for over a year, and she hated the place. She especially hated the cutesy uniforms the waitresses were required to wear—red T-shirts that had their names spelled out in blue lettering across the back, short cheerleader-style skirts, and saddle shoes.

At lunchtime the place was jammed with office workers from the nearby buildings and housewives out shopping at the department stores. The worst were the harried mothers who came, toddlers in tow, to meet their friends. They sat and gossiped for hours, ordered the kids gooey ice cream concoctions that glopped all over the tables, and left chintzy tips.

So far this shift, Sarah had been pulling mostly tables of men. That was just the way she liked it. The men ordered hefty lunches that they ate in a hurry because they had to get back to work, they left good tips, and they didn't keep calling her back for extra napkins, straws, or another glass of Coke "because this one just spilled."

On the other hand, they had big mouths that sometimes she felt like punching. Like the guy at the front booth, showing off for his friends.

He leered at her when she brought him his medium-well chili burger and said, "I love those outfits, don't you? Looks a little big on you, honey."

Sarah ignored him and sorted out the rest of the orders—two bacon burgers with the works and a tuna cheese melt with a side of fried onions.

The television over the bar at the front of the

restaurant was turned loud enough that it could be heard above the noisy conversations and the clatter of the dishes. Sometimes customers asked that the volume be lowered because, they complained, they couldn't hear themselves speak.

But the manager insisted that the sound be turned up. He said it made the place feel lively even when business was slow. Sarah had learned to tune it out, like elevator music.

The newscaster came on with the one o'clock news break. She flashed a toothy grin into the camera and read the top story. "All three men accused of raping a young woman at a local bar were released today on ten thousand dollars' bail."

Hearing the word "rape," Sarah looked up just in time to catch the rest of the sentence.

The customer with the chili burger tapped her on the arm. "Honey," he complained, "this isn't well-done." He held up his plate to show her. "This is barely cooked."

"Lawyers for the accused men," the newscaster continued, "felt confident that facts may reveal the young woman wasn't raped."

Sarah stared at the television set, frozen with disbelief.

"Honey, it's raw," the customer repeated.

Sarah didn't hear his complaint. Her mind was riveted on the newcaster's words: *"Facts may reveal that the young woman wasn't raped."*

Bob Joiner's frat brothers put on a keg of beer as soon as Bob returned from the courthouse with the good news about his bail. Now they were toasting his victory in front of the television, watching the same newscast as Sarah, and hoping to catch some footage of Bob and his codefendants. Bob appreciated his friend's support, but he wished they would quit making him out to be some kind of celebrity.

Philip Joyce stood at the back of the room, feeling increasingly angry and ashamed. If only he had the guts to say to Bob, *How could you do a thing like that?*

His stomach turned every time he thought about that girl lying on the pinball machine. His frat brothers' remarks about Sarah Tobias and what they would like to do to her disgusted him.

But who was he to talk? He was no better than Bob. So he hadn't touched her himself. Big deal. But he had stood by and watched while they all took their turns with Sarah, and he hadn't done a damn thing to stop them.

And now the guys were making a hero out of Bob. Clapping him on the back for "showing the world what fraternity boys were made of." Shouting, "Speech, speech—c'mon, Joiner, give us a speech."

The newscast cut to a shot of George Henley, standing in the hallway just outside the courtroom, facing a sea of mikes.

"Our defense is simple," Henley declared, pausing for dramatic emphasis. "There *was* no rape. The so-called victim consented, enthusiastically, to all of the alleged acts. She put on a show, pure and simple."

When the camera panned to Bob, standing between his father and Henley, his friends broke into loud applause and laughter and pulled Bob to his feet to take a bow.

Their cheers reminded Philip of the commotion and clamor at the Mill. Suddenly, he had to get out of that room, away from all the noise and celebration. As he stood up to leave, his eyes met Bob's. His friend threw him a look that pleaded for understanding.

Philip turned and headed upstairs. The thing of it was, he couldn't understand—not Bob nor himself, either.

The party broke up after a few drinks. Bob grabbed a couple of beers and went up to his room. As he had expected, Philip was there, hunched in front of the computer, working on his paper.

He set one of the beers down in front of Philip, who wordlessly nodded his thanks. Then he grabbed his sweats out of the closet.

"Coming to practice?" he asked.

"No," Philip muttered. "I've got to finish this."

"I don't think they know you were there," Bob said casually. "And I didn't tell them. I said to myself, why put my friend Philip on the spot? He'd never do that to me."

He paused, then continued as if it were an afterthought, "They haven't called you, have they?"

Philip shook his head no.

"Not that it matters. What could you say?" He grinned, remembering. "That she put on a great show, right?"

"Show? It kinda looked like—"

"Philip, she was begging for it," Bob said with absolute assurance.

Philip turned back to the computer.

"I ought to charge you rent on that."

"I can borrow somebody else's," Philip said tightly.

Bob slung his bookbag over his shoulder and tapped Philip on the back. "Hey, lighten up, Philip," he laughed. "I'm heckling you."

Katheryn and Dunc went back to the Mill on Tuesday. Sarah had told them that one of the waitresses there, Sally Frazer, was a friend of hers. She had been working on Saturday night, and Sarah thought maybe she might have seen something. Dunc had a few more questions he wanted to throw at Jesse, so he cornered him at the bar, while Katheryn interviewed Sally in the game room.

Sally had curly red hair, which she wore short and fluffy, and a friendly, open face that turned suspicious as soon as Katheryn introduced herself.

"I'm trying to help Sarah," Katheryn explained. But Sally still looked wary.

"She said you were here that night," Katheryn said pointedly.

Sally shrugged. Okay, if that's what Sarah wanted . . .

Katheryn set up her tape recorder and asked Sally, for the record, whether it was true that she had been present at the Mill the night Sarah was attacked.

"Yeah, I was here, but I didn't see what happened. But if Sarah says she was raped, she was raped."

"Can you identify any of the men who assaulted her?" asked Katheryn.

"No. I was out there." She pointed toward the bar. "Besides, these guys were blocking the doorway, so I really couldn't see, and anyway my shift was over, so I left while she was still in here."

"Did you know any of these guys who were blocking your view?"

Sally shook her head. "Uh-uh. They were gettin' real rowdy, yellin' and clappin', and I really thought she was just partyin', ya know?"

"Can you describe any of them?"

"Like how?"

"Did you notice anything different about any of them—like long hair, a beard, a moustache, a birthmark, a bandanna." Katheryn kept fishing, hoping to jog Sally's memory. "Jewelry—an earring, a scar, a tattoo—"

Pay dirt.

"A tattoo," Sally said slowly. "Yeah."

"Can you describe it?"

"A scorpion. This one guy had a scorpion."

"How many drinks would you say Sarah had had?"

"I don't know." Sally shrugged her shoulders. "She was pretty loaded. She just had this big fight with Larry—this guy she lives with? And she really just wanted to cool out a little."

"What do you know about Larry?"

"Not much, except that he's an asshole. I mean, he says he's a musician, but he's really just a dealer. He rides a motorcycle."

Terrific. George Henley would have a field day on the witness stand with this crew. Katheryn hoped that Dunc was having better luck with Jesse than she was here.

"C'mon, Jesse," she could hear Dunc saying. "Don't jerk me off. You've worked here a long time, and this dump gets a lot of regulars. Who?"

"Look, it was Saturday night—a real mob. You think I got time to look at faces?"

Dunc gestured with his hand—don't jerk me off—and raised a skeptical eyebrow.

"C'mon, man," Jesse pleaded, cracking his knuckles. "These guys are my bread and butter."

"You sure you don't remember anyone else?"

"There was some kid I never seen before. Played one of the video machines all night."

"Who was with him?"

"Nobody I saw."

Dunc stood up and took a long, thoughtful look at the row of liquor bottles lined up behind Jesse. "Well," he said casually, "I guess I'm gonna have to call the State Liquor Authority and tell 'em how you kept right on serving up the booze while they were committing a violent felony."

Katheryn joined him at the bar. "Ready?" she said.

"Yup." He turned back to the angry bartender. "Thanks, Jesse. We'll talk."

He held the door for Katheryn, as she took one last, quick look at the game room, with its row of video machines blinking across the space at her.

If machines could only talk, she would have all the answers she needed.

Jesse waited until they were outside and gone before he poured himself a much-needed shot of whiskey. He threw it down in one gulp, then succinctly expressed himself on the subject of Detective Duncan.

"Scumbag."

CHAPTER SEVEN

CONNIE HARDING WAS ABOUT THE LAST PERSON in the world Katheryn wanted to find in the lobby of her apartment building. Her sister had stationed herself next to the doorman's desk. She was perched on top of a battered-looking suitcase, surrounded by more suitcases and bulging cardboard cartons tied together with rope.

"What is this?" Katheryn snapped, trying to keep her voice from rising to a scream.

Connie stood up, scattering cigarette ashes all over the floor. "This guy wouldn't let me in," she said, pouting.

"He's not supposed to." Katheryn pretended not to see her neighbors' stares as they passed through the lobby. What could they be thinking of Connie, who, as usual, looked like a poster girl for the Hell's Angels? If she was lucky, they might take her for one of Katheryn's clients.

The doorman cleared his throat uneasily. This girl who claimed to be Miss Murphy's sister had been giving him a hard time for the last two hours. He wanted her and all her junk out of the lobby before anyone complained.

"You said to give her an envelope, but you didn't say anything about letting her into your place," he reminded Katheryn.

"I understand," Katheryn said, furious with Connie for humiliating her in front of her doorman.

"I'm your sister, for God's sake," Connie announced loudly.

As if I could ever forget. Her teeth clenched, Katheryn said, "I left you a check."

"I told you, I don't want charity." Connie handed the envelope with the check to Katheryn and bent down to pick up her suitcases. "Can you get those boxes?"

"And do what?"

"Bring them upstairs."

"Connie," said Katheryn, emphasizing each word, "you're not moving in here."

Connie stared at her like a petulant child. "I couldn't find anything. Besides, a couple of days won't kill you."

"This is not a couple of days. What's wrong with your eye?" she said, suddenly noticing that Connie had an ugly bruise.

"I tripped. What's your problem? Look," Connie said angrily. "I have just been left by a boyfriend of several years—"

"Probably because he was tired of supporting you," Katheryn lashed out. Instantly, she regretted her words.

"Katheryn?" It was David, come to collect her for dinner.

She whirled around, furious that he should have caught her in the middle of this family soap opera.

David stared at Connie, who was dressed in a low-cut tank top and tight jeans. But all he said was, "Ready?"

"In a minute," Katheryn said with a grim smile.

She turned back to Connie in time to see her sister throw David a glance whose meaning was all too obvious.

"Hello," David said, wondering what the relationship was between this pretty, stacked girl and Katheryn, who seemed uncharacteristically rattled.

Katheryn sighed. She had to save face with David—and Connie knew it.

"One night, Connie, that's it," she said coldly.

"You're a real piece of work, Katheryn," Connie retorted, a triumphant smile lighting her face.

David pointed to Connie's baggage. "What's all this?" he asked.

"My life," Katheryn said sourly.

"Anything I can do to help?"

"Careful, she'll take you up on it." Katheryn shuddered at the thought of David getting an earful from her sister.

"He's cute," Connie mouthed behind David's back.

Katheryn ignored her. "Shall we go?"

"Don't keep my sister out too late," Connie called after them.

Katheryn could have strangled her.

The telephone shrilled. On the third ring, Sarah decided to answer it.

"Hello?" she said, her eyes glued to the television set. "Where are you? . . . No, Larry . . . Because I don't *want* to go out . . . Then I'll see you after . . . Okay, 'bye."

A couple of minutes later, someone knocked at her door.

"Who is it?" she called, wishing they'd go away so she could watch her program.

"Katheryn Murphy."

Piss off, thought Sarah. She stayed where she was and continued watching her favorite soap heroine, who was trying to escape through the snow from a crazed maniac with a killer attack dog.

The program cut to a commercial.

Sarah slowly walked over to the door, opened it a crack, and stood blocking the threshold.

"So why did you let them out on bail?" she demanded.

"I didn't let them out," Katheryn said calmly. "It's standard procedure. Until a jury finds you guilty, you're free if you can post bail."

"The guy on TV made it sound like I did a live sex show."

"That won't be the last time that happens. Can I come in?"

Sarah grudgingly moved out of the way.

"The bartender at the Dugout said you were sick."

"I had to go to the doctor. See, nobody at work knows about it." The thought of Katheryn nosing around at the Dugout, asking questions, made her nervous. She had nothing to hide, but her private business was just that—private.

The bottle of tequila on the kitchen table was just what she wanted to calm herself down. "Want a drink or something?" she offered. "I could sure use a drink."

"No, thanks." Katheryn stepped inside and looked around. She took in the unwashed dishes piled in the sink and the papers and candy wrappers strewn on the floor around the bed.

Sarah could feel her making a connection between the disorder and the bottle of tequila in her hand. *Screw it,* she decided and poured herself a shot.

"It's just to smooth out the edges," she assured Katheryn. Then she remembered what she had meant to ask Katheryn the next time she saw her. "Listen, do you know what time you were born?"

"Look, I really don't believe in horoscopes," Katheryn said wearily.

"But I do," Sarah persisted. "What time?"

"At night. Seven at night. August sixth."

"Where?"

Katheryn removed a stack of laundry from one of the chairs and sat down. "Portland. Do you always drink to smooth out the edges?"

"Sometimes I smoke pot," said Sarah defiantly. "You want some?"

"No, thanks."

Sadie wandered over to Katheryn, sniffed her shoe, and wagged her tail, begging to be petted.

"Sadie get outta here," scolded Sarah, shooing the dog away. She shrugged apologetically at Katheryn. "She likes visitors."

Katheryn set her tape recorder on the table. She switched it on and got straight to the point of her visit. "Did you drink anything before you went to the Mill? Or smoke anything?"

Sarah shrugged. "Half a joint, maybe, and a couple of beers. Nothing heavy."

"And while you were there?"

"I dunno—I wasn't fallin' down, just loose."

"How were you dressed?"

"What's that supposed to mean?" She stared at Katheryn, thinking, *Where the hell does she come off?*

"Were you dressed provocatively?" Katheryn continued, ignoring Sarah's question. "I mean, like a lot of cleavage, a see-through blouse?"

Sarah's voice rose. "What the fuck difference does it matter how I was dressed? They tore it off me."

"But did how you were dressed make those guys think they could have sex with you? Did you put on a show?"

"What are you talking about?" Sarah exploded. "You saw me at the hospital. You think I asked for that? If that's what you think, get the fuck out of my house!!"

Katheryn sat back in the chair and acted as if she hadn't heard a word of Sarah's explosion. She said calmly, "Why didn't you tell me you had a record?"

Sarah froze. After a moment, she said, "Oh fuck . . ."

"I beg your pardon?"

"It's not *my* record, okay?"

"So whose is it? Larry's?"

"No. I mean, yeah, he's got a record, but I didn't know him then. He's cleaned up his act and—"

Katheryn interrupted her. "We're not talking about Larry. We're talking about you. Want to tell me about it?"

Sarah sat down on the edge of the bed, stunned that Katheryn had dug up that ancient information. What else, she wondered, had this nosy bitch found out about her?

Trying not to allow her anger and discomfort to show, Sarah said, "I was helping a friend move, a girlfriend in Chicago. I was driving the U-Haul with her desk in it, and a cop stopped me because the brake lights were broken. He searched the truck and found a little coke in one of the drawers. *Her* drawer in *her* desk."

"Then why is it still on the books?"

"I don't know. The charges were definitely dropped. Hey," she protested indignantly, "check it out if you don't believe me."

"Have you ever made love to more than one man at a time?" Katheryn asked calmly.

"What the fuck kind of question is that?" screamed Sarah. She jumped up, looking as if she were about to take a swing at Katheryn.

Katheryn sighed and turned off the tape recorder.

"It's the kind of question you're going to be asked on the stand."

She began ticking off the items on her fingers. "You're also going to be asked if Larry—or any other man—has ever hit you, and if you liked it. You're going to be asked about your coke bust, and about how many drinks a day you take to smooth out the edges, and how many joints."

Sarah leaned forward, as if to stop her.

But Katheryn silenced her with a stern look and continued the catechism. "How often you go to bars alone, whether you wear underwear when you go to them, and which diseases you've caught and how many abortions you've had. And I'm going to object to all those questions, and sometimes the judge is going to sustain me—but sometimes not."

"That's not right," Sarah said, bewildered.

"Sarah, you're a witness, and the defense's job is to show the jury that you're a rotten witness because you have a rotten character."

Sarah fought back her tears. She shouted, "So I'm just a low-class asshole, and you won't defend me, right?"

"Wrong," Katheryn replied calmly. "I didn't say that."

Sarah didn't get this woman at all. Katheryn was as cold as ice, and she was full of ugly questions, and she looked at her as if Sarah were a piece of dog turd. And then she turned around and said, yeah, sure, she would defend her.

But hell, Sarah decided, pouring herself another

shot of tequila, Katheryn didn't have to *like* her. All she had to do was fight for her. And it was her job. "Will those bastards go to jail?" she finally asked.

"Is that what you want?"

"I want to put those fuckers away."

Katheryn stared silently at Sarah, thinking, *You still don't get what this trial will be like for you.*

It would be the ugliest, worst kind of show. Henley and his buddies would dig up all the dirt on Sarah, and by the time they were finished smearing it all over her reputation, the jury would be ready to convict *her* instead of the three defendants.

And if the case went to trial, there wasn't a damn thing Katheryn could do to stop them. And no way could she get Sarah to understand that. She wished she liked Sarah, or at least had more sympathy for her. But most of all, she wished she hadn't answered the damn phone on Saturday night.

Attending hockey games with the district attorney was a hallowed office tradition. Those tapped by Paul Rudolph to join him for an evening at the hockey stadium knew they were, if only temporarily, one of the chosen—"one of the guys." Katheryn Murphy was the first woman deputy D.A. to make it to that exalted rank.

Fortunately she understood the sport. She admired the way the players raced across the ice in pursuit of the puck. And she could hold her own debating the merits of the various players.

This evening Rudolph had also invited Al Massi, a

hardworking, meticulous, but unimaginative deputy D.A. Although his play-it-safe philosophy frequently irritated Katheryn, she nevertheless respected his intelligence and liked his company.

She was looking forward to the game. At lunchtime she had skimmed the sports page. This looked to be a good match.

They had hoped to get there before the end of the first period. But, as usual, Paul was running late and couldn't find the tickets. When Katheryn and Al came to collect him in his office—decorated with photographs of Paul and the governor, the state senators, and other important politicians—he was frantically rummaging through his desk drawers.

Katheryn rapped sharply on the open door. "Paul—game time!"

"One second, one second," he mumbled. He straightened up and looked at them helplessly. "Where the hell are the tickets?"

Al reached into his jacket pocket and produced the three tickets. "You gave them to me to hold," he said with a flourish.

Rudolph shook his head at his forgetfulness and grabbed his coat. "Where are you on the Tobias case?" he asked Katheryn as they headed toward the elevators.

"At the game," Katheryn promised. "Come on! You know what parking is like over there."

They made it to the stadium with time enough to buy dinner—hot dogs, pizza, and beers. As the sports columnists had predicted, the two teams were well matched, and emotions were running high, both on and off the ice.

In between haranguing the ref for his stupid calls, Paul and Al debated with Katheryn the merits of plea bargaining Sarah's case.

"If I take it to trial," Katheryn argued, one eye on the ice, "they'll destroy her. She walked in there alone, she got drunk, she got stoned, she came on to them, she's got a prior for possession—"

"That's inadmissible," Al reminded her.

"Sure, it's inadmissible. But they'll ask her about it. I'll object, the judge will sustain me—but the jury will hear it. She's a sitting duck."

Al finished his hot dog and wiped the mustard off his lips. "I read her Q-and-A. It's an ugly case."

"Al, I know it's an ugly case. The question is whether it's a winnable case."

On the ice a pitched battle had erupted among the players. Hockey sticks, arms, legs, anything that could move was called into action as a weapon. The refs skated helplessly around the combatants, as the fans, inflamed with excitement, shouted encouragement. They egged their teams on with cries of "Kill the bastard" and "Get 'em good this time."

When the officials had finally sorted out the teams and assigned two players to the penalty box, Paul resumed the discussion. "Katheryn," he said good-naturedly, "we all understand you love to win, but I can't let you dismiss just because you don't have a lock."

'Lock? I don't have a *case,"* she protested loudly. "Her girlfriend didn't see anything. The bartender didn't see anything. The others either didn't see anything or were too drunk or didn't think anything special was going on. I've got Polito, and the moment the defense brings out that he's on probation, they'll show we squeezed him, and he's worthless."

"What about the guy who called—the one with the conscience?" asked Paul, offering her his box of popcorn.

She shook her head. "We've got his voice on tape, but we don't know who he is or where to look for him."

Paul took a last swig of beer and emptied the paper cup. "Do you believe she was raped?"

"Yes," Katheryn said slowly. "But Paul, I'm telling you, I can't win this case."

"They can't walk," Paul said firmly. "Make a deal and put them away."

"Make a deal? With *what?"*

"You've got enough. Try for rape two."

Katheryn laughed mirthlessly.

"Okay," he conceded. "Any felony. If you can get a violent one—assault, coercion, reckless endangerment, menacing—even better."

"Paul, I don't see—"

"Katheryn, you said she was raped. So make a deal and put them away. I don't care if you only get them six months in county. But *put them away."*

As if to underscore his command, the crowd roared

in response to yet another, even more violent clash between the two teams.

"Kill 'em, kill 'em!" screamed the fans.

The home-team goalie looked up and brandished his stick at the audience.

The crowd went for blood. "Make 'em pay!" they chanted. "Make 'em pay!"

CHAPTER EIGHT

KATHERYN WATCHED CONNIE MAKE A HALF-hearted attempt to pick up the apartment. Dirty plates and cups were stacked haphazardly in the sink. An empty TV-dinner tray sat on the counter that separated the kitchen from the dining room. Beer bottles were scattered around the living room.

Connie was still dressed in the filmy lime-green nightgown she'd had on that morning when Katheryn left the apartment.

"I didn't feel good," she said despondently when Katheryn got home from work.

Katheryn, on the other hand, was feeling more cheerful than she had since the moment Connie had invaded her lobby. She had devoted a couple of hours that morning to going through the newspaper classified ads and making some calls.

The result had been well worth her efforts. Connie was tolerable in very limited doses. But Katheryn wasn't the type to have a roommate, especially not Connie.

But her announcement that she had found Connie a reasonably priced apartment didn't seem to improve Connie's spirits.

"I'm not bothering you," she said bitterly. "What do you care if I hang out here for a while longer?"

Katheryn ignored her objections and proceeded to phone the landlord to confirm the rental.

"Thanks very much," she told the landlord. "We'll be over in half an hour."

She hung up and handed Connie the piece of paper with all the information.

"First and last months are paid. Utilities are covered, and there's a phone in the hall until you get your own."

"You want an award or a commission?" Connie scowled.

"Just get your clothes on, okay? I think you'll like it."

"I told you," Connie complained, "I can't be alone right now."

"Connie, I cannot stay home and take care of you."

They glared at each other, fighting to wound, as in the old days.

"All you learned at school was to make people believe it doesn't hurt when you knife them in the back," Connie said angrily.

"Look," said Katheryn, stung by the accusation and going for blood herself. "I don't want a roommate who acts like a horny teenager every time she meets a man."

Connie grabbed the paper out of Katheryn's hand. "Don't give me any of that judgment crap," she shouted, turning the volume up in stages. "We grew up in the same house, remember? You can go fuck yourself, Miss Deputy D.A. asshole."

She stormed into the bathroom and slammed the door behind her.

Katheryn ignored her temper tantrum. Connie would come around eventually—she had no other choice. She would agree to look at the apartment, and then she would agree to rent it, with Katheryn's help, of course.

Katheryn would have her own life back again, without any of Connie's mess to come home to. She yanked open the dishwasher and began loading it with the dirty dishes Connie had left in the sink.

Paul had said, "Make a deal."

Okay, she would make a deal. But Paul would owe her an Oscar for the performance she was about to give to convince the defense attorneys that she had something to bargain with.

Dunc had persuaded Arthur Polito—how, Katheryn didn't ask—to consent to be interviewed on videotape. His responses were grudging but adequate.

Henley, Dalton, and Sklar agreed to a Saturday-morning meeting with her and Al Massi. Confident that Katheryn would want to plea bargain, they arrived in high spirits, ready to do business.

Dalton and Sklar had made a date to play golf at one o'clock, and they were eager to get the matter settled quickly. Katheryn gave them a few minutes to review the contents of the file on Sarah's case: transcripts of the witnesses' interviews, copies of the medical reports, large blowups of the photos taken of Sarah at the hospital.

Then she showed them the videotape of her Arthur Polito interview.

"You understand, Mr. Polito," she could be heard questioning him off-camera, "that you'll be testifying before a grand jury and at a trial?"

"Yeah," Polito replied sullenly. "I get that."

"And that you'll be testifying against people you know?"

"Yeah."

"Mr. Polito, have I or anyone in my office or Detective Duncan, or anyone in the police department, offered you any inducement to testify—money, gifts, anything at all?"

"Nah." Polito grimaced.

"Have I or anyone threatened or coerced you in any way?"

Again, "Nah."

"Thank you, Mr. Polito."

The image went to gray static, and Al turned off the set.

"He's just a taste," Katheryn told the three defense lawyers, wondering how much of her story they were prepared to buy. "The bar was filled with witnesses, and we anticipate that they'll testify for the people."

Dalton called her bluff. "You anticipate? A hundred says you'll have to drag them into court."

Sklar chuckled. "Another hundred says they'll be useless because they were too drunk."

"Whatever you say." Katheryn smiled.

"Keep in mind that under the law we don't need corroboration to prove rape," Al reminded the three of them.

"And we do have medical evidence," Katheryn said, pointing to the medical reports. "No doubt about penetration. And physical evidence. No doubt about force."

"What will you take?" asked Dalton.

Katheryn had rehearsed this earlier with Al. Now, without a moment's hesitation, she said, "Rape one."

Gesturing with his head to indicate he was speaking on behalf of his colleagues as well, Dalton said, "We were thinking more in the line of, say, sexual abuse two."

"Rape one," Katheryn repeated. She laughed derisively. "Maybe I can convince the judge not to give them the maximum."

Dalton stood up. "I'd rather go to trial."

"Fine," shrugged Katheryn, gathering her papers. "Oh, by the way, no separate deals. One goes to trial, all go to trial."

Henley and Sklar glanced at each other.

"What would you say to . . . sexual abuse one?" Sklar suggested.

"I'd say rape one."

"Katheryn, cut the crap," Dalton broke in angrily. "Your Polito looks about as strong as a wet Kleenex. If you had anybody better, you'd have showed us his tape. And your complaining witness—ugh! She walked into a bar, got loaded and stoned, and did everything but yank their dicks. No jury'll buy her."

Katheryn smiled dismissively, though Dalton's point was well taken. But she had played this game many times before and walked away with the prize. Poker-faced, she waited for their next offer.

Exasperated and showing it, Dalton asked, "What would you say to rape two with a recommendation for . . . one year?"

"I'd say go to hell."

George Henley cleared his throat. He said, "Miss Murphy, are you sure you're in a position to be quite so . . . shall we say adamant? A rape trial is—"

"Always a gamble," Katheryn broke in, still smiling. "I agree, Mr. Henley. And I know your reputation. But look at the pictures. That's what the jury's going to see. And they're going to see the girl, too. You can't tell it from these pictures, Mr. Henley, but she's tiny. She's the most defenseless-looking thing you ever saw. If we go to trial and you lose, I will ask for . . ." She paused and looked at each of them in turn. "Fifteen to twenty-five. And I'll get it."

Sklar spoke up for the first time. "Eighteen months," he offered.

"Stop dancing," Katheryn said impatiently.

"What's your best offer?" asked Dalton.

"Two to five on rape two. With luck, your boys are out in nine months, and that's a gift."

A silent signal flashed among the three lawyers.

"On one condition," Henley said.

She knew she had won. "Condition?"

"I'll accept that on behalf of my client if the formal charge is changed to one without a sexual element. He's twenty-two, he's an A student, he's got a future."

"I can't do that," Katheryn said flatly.

Henley shook his head. This last point was a deal breaker. "He won't plead guilty to a sexual offense."

"Let's see," Katheryn said, reluctantly riffling through the pages of her penal code volume. "Violent felonies . . . assault . . . coercion . . . reckless endangerment . . ."

"Reckless endangerment." Henley could live with that.

Katheryn could, too. An indictment for reckless endangerment was much better than she had hoped for.

She looked questioningly at Sklar and Dalton. They hesitated momentarily, almost pro forma, then nodded their agreement.

The meeting ended quickly after that. The big-gun defense attorneys had been bested, and they knew it. They packed up their briefcases, shook hands, and went off to break the news to their clients.

Al kept silent until they were well out of the room, the door firmly shut behind them. But his gloating grin betrayed his satisfaction. As soon as he was sure they were out of earshot, he turned to Katheryn and raised his hand for a high five.

Katheryn slapped him back.

"Two to five!" she said triumphantly. "Two to five!"

CHAPTER NINE

PHILIP JOYCE WORKED FIVE AFTERNOONS A WEEK in the school cafeteria. The job and his course load left him little free time. But his tuition and board were a burden for his parents, and the money he earned meant he could cover the rest of his expenses.

The job was boring but undemanding. Philip usually spent the hours in the cafeteria daydreaming about girls.

But ever since that Saturday night, he had been struggling not only with his conscience but with the unaccustomed feeling that he *should* have done more. He *should* have tried to stop Bob, *should* have pulled him away from Sarah Tobias.

And there was one thing he *should* be doing now—*could* still do to help her case against Bob and the others.

Except that stepping forward and admitting that he

had been present at the Mill that night would mean betraying his best friend.

Today the cafeteria was quiet except for the music coming from the kitchen. It had rained earlier in the day, a soft, misty rain, but then the clouds had rolled away and the sky had suddenly cleared. Now the sun streaming through the windows felt good on his back and face as he moved from table to table, stacking dirty lunch trays onto the portable rack.

He finished up in the students' cafeteria, then moved next door to the faculty lounge. At this hour of the late afternoon the lounge was empty except for two teachers at a corner table, gossiping over coffee. Absorbed in the latest tenure battle, they were as oblivious to Philip as they were to the sound of the television, tuned to the early edition of the news.

Tonight's top story, the anchorman announced, concerned the latest developments in the recent rape of a local woman.

"Lawyers for the defendants refused to comment on the rape two plea bargain. But the office of District Attorney Paul Rudolph stated that the horror of the victim's experience made her ill equipped to take the stand and be a strong witness in a rigorous trial. The defendants each received a minimum sentence and could be out in six months, depending on an appeal. Coming up—a look at sports." The program cut to a commercial.

Philip stared blankly at the screen, blind to the shot of a young woman in the shower, singing the praises of her deodorant.

His mind was on the newscaster's words: ". . . the horror of the victim's experience . . ."

The horror he had witnessed.

But now he could stop castigating himself for not admitting that he had been at the Mill. He could stop worrying about having to point a finger at Bob.

The matter had been settled by the lawyers. To spare the girl. And, in the end, wasn't that what was most important?

From the kitchen, where Katheryn was arranging the scampi and mushroom rice on a serving platter, she could hear that her dinner party for Ted Millbank, his partners, and their wives, was going beautifully. David came in with the dirty salad plates.

"Where do I put these?" he asked.

"On the sink. And can you open the white wine?"

He reached for the corkscrew just as the doorbell rang. David threw her a quizzical glance.

Katheryn said, "Will you get that, David?" And thought, *No, please, not Connie.*

The uninvited guest turned out to be not Connie but Sarah Tobias, come straight from work in her waitress uniform.

"You goddamn bitch! You sold me out!" she exploded.

Katheryn stared at her, astonished. "Sarah—"

"Did you see this?" Sarah brandished the newspaper she was clutching in one hand. "This is what you did!"

Recovering her composure, Katheryn said, "Sarah, you can't just—"

Sarah paid no attention to her. She punched the newspaper again and again as she loudly repeated what she had read about herself in the paper: "I wouldn't make a good witness, I'm too fragile, my past is questionable, I'm a drunk, I'm a dope addict, I'm a slut who got bounced around a little in a bar—and I wasn't raped!"

"Of course you were raped. You—"

"Then why doesn't it say so here? Why doesn't it say they *raped* Sarah Tobias? What the fuck is *reckless endangerment?*"

Katheryn glanced apologetically at her guests, then said firmly, "Reckless endangerment is a violent felony that carries the same prison term as rape. You told me you wanted me to put them away, and I put them away. Now why don't you—"

But Sarah was not about to be mollified. "According to the fuckin' paper, I'm a liar," she shouted. "Nobody raped me, nothing happened. Who the hell are you to decide I'm not good enough to be a witness? I bet if I went to law school and didn't live in a fuckin' trailer, I'd be good enough. Lady . . . you suck shit!"

"Sarah, believe me," Katheryn said, her voice like ice. "That's the best I could—"

Sarah slammed her fist against the table. "God damn you!" she raged. "My pants were down, my crotch was hung out there for the whole world to see, three guys were sticking it to me, a bunch of others were cheering and clapping—and *you* stand there telling me that's the best you could do?"

She was too wound up to notice David edging toward her. "Well, your best sucks," she shouted, "and so do you. I don't know what you got out of selling me out, lady, but I sure as shit hope it was worth it."

"Okay, that's enough," David said quietly. He grabbed her shoulder and began to push her toward the door.

"Get your hands off me . . . get your fuckin' hands off me!" she yelled, struggling to pull away from his grasp.

"David, let her go!" shouted Katheryn. "Let her go, goddamnit!"

Sarah flung her newspaper at Katheryn. Then, without another word, she walked out and slammed the door behind her.

She didn't for one minute regret walking in on Katheryn Murphy and her fancy-pants boyfriend and guests. She'd noticed them all staring at her, like she was some kind of crazy woman. But hell, hadn't Katheryn already made her out to be much worse than crazy? It didn't hurt for them to know that when they played God up there in their fancy offices, they were screwing up people's lives.

Real people, like Sarah Tobias.

And she didn't need that kind of shit.

As usual, Larry wasn't home, which was fine, because she didn't feel like looking at his ugly face. But Sadie scampered over and begged for attention. Sarah hugged her until the dog squirmed.

She wandered aimlessly around the trailer, moving from the bed to the kitchen to the bathroom. Usually, the size of the trailer didn't bother her. It was the first place she had ever lived in that felt as if it were *her* home, not a place she dropped into or out of at a moment's whim. But tonight it felt cramped and confining, as if she had overstayed her welcome there and it was time to move on.

One thing was for sure: she needed some kind of change.

Catching sight of herself in the bathroom mirror, Sarah came to a sudden decision. She quickly picked up a pair of scissors and snipped off a piece of her long blond hair. The scissors snapped again, and another hank of hair fell to the floor . . . and another . . . and then another.

Intent on trimming the sides, she didn't notice the bathroom door open until she saw Larry's reflection in the mirror. He was staring at her as if she were crazy.

"What are you doin'?" he asked.

"I need a change." Not that it was any of his business.

He squinted at her and said, "It looks kind of weird."

Sarah spun around angrily.

"Hey." He held up his hands to signal peace. "Nothin' heavy. I'm just not used to it."

She turned around and started cutting again, then stopped and glared at him. "Get out."

Larry frowned. "Shit, man, cut it any way you like."

"Get out. Get out of here."

"Okay. I'll see you later." He shrugged.

"No," Sarah said. "I mean *out*. Get out, and don't fuckin' come back."

"Bullshit."

"This is my place, and I don't want you in it. Now—get out."

He was about to argue with her. But then he saw how her hand was wrapped so tightly around the scissors that her knuckles were white.

He held up his middle finger—*fuck you*—and took off.

Sarah slammed the door shut behind him and put her head down on the edge of the sink.

Oh, God, she thought. *I've really done it now.*

Katheryn sat in her bedroom touching up her makeup. Her guests, except for David, had left. Soft music was playing on the stereo in the living room. *Mood music.*

"Hey." David tapped lightly on the bathroom door. "I'm getting lonesome out here."

Her hand trembled, and a smudge of green eye shadow appeared above her brow.

She put down the brush, picked it up again. Then, with a last, bemused look at herself in the mirror, she put it back in its case and walked into the living room.

"Hi there," David said softly, reaching for her.

She smiled weakly and said, "David, would you be upset if I asked you to go?"

"Upset? Hmm . . . disappointed," he said with a wry expression on his face.

"I'm sorry. I just can't . . . My head is someplace else right now."

"What is it? Your crazy client? Maybe I should sue her for ruining our night."

Katheryn laughed sourly. "Don't bother. She doesn't have a dime. Look, it's not your fault. I'd . . . I'd just like to be alone."

He could see there was no point in trying to change her mind. "Okay," he conceded, taking her hand and pulling her close to him.

An awkward moment passed between them as they tacitly acknowledged that they had expected this night to end differently.

With a good-humored shrug, he gave her a friendly good-night kiss and was gone.

If Katheryn had had to explain just then why she wanted David to leave, whether Sarah Tobias had anything to do with her need to sleep alone that night, she would have been hard pressed to come up with an answer. She so rarely permitted herself the luxury of confusion that she had no experience sifting through her emotions and sorting out her motives.

But she did know that what she was feeling just now added up to an unfamiliar and disquieting sense that the natural order of her universe had been disrupted.

CHAPTER TEN

SARAH COULDN'T QUITE GET USED TO NOT HAVING hair bouncing against the back of her neck. The shorter style made her feel different—freer, lighter, less encumbered.

She had done a good night's work.

On Monday morning, to reward herself, she stopped at the record store on her way to work to buy some new tapes.

Checking the cassette bin, she suddenly got the feeling that someone was watching her. She looked up. A nice-looking guy, in his early thirties, dressed in jeans and a leather jacket, was staring at her.

"You caught me. Sorry." He grinned.

Jerk. She smiled stiffly, acknowledging his apology.

"Listen," he said, "this is gonna sound like the worst kind of crap, but I've seen you some—"

"You're right," she interrupted. "The worst kind of crap."

"Was it in a bar?"

"I used to work at the Dugout."

The guy took another long look at her. "No, it wasn't there. Did you used to have long hair? Not real long, but longer?"

"No," she said abruptly. She picked out the two cassettes she wanted and walked quickly to the cash register.

He trailed along behind her. "What shifts do you work?" he asked.

"Look," Sarah said, annoyed, "I live with somebody."

"Hey, I don't mind." The man laughed.

"I do." She grabbed the tapes and zipped up her jacket.

Still trying to place her, the man followed her out of the store and toward her car. And then he put it together—the yellow Camaro, the familiar license plate, "SXY SADI."

He whistled loudly and said, "Now I remember."

"You got me mixed up with somebody," Sarah said angrily.

"Nah, it's you. Sexy Sadi. You were that girl at the Mill, right?"

That girl at the Mill. Her cheeks flamed with the humiliation of having been recognized—her worst nightmare come true.

She quickly got into the car, locked the doors, and fumbled for her keys. She didn't see the man gesture at her obscenely.

Screw you, she swore silently. She ground the key

into the ignition and flooded the engine in her eagerness to get out of the parking lot and away from this creep. A second try, and she managed to get the car started.

A horn beeped . . . beeped again.

He was sitting behind the wheel of his Toyota, parked just in front of her, grinning like an asshole, wiggling his tongue suggestively, moving his hand up and down, his meaning all too obvious.

"Wanna play some pinball?" he yelled, and he began to laugh as if he'd just cracked the joke of the century.

Sarah came out swinging, her simmering anger boiling over into white-hot rage. She smashed her foot down on the gas pedal, and her car careened forward, slamming the Toyota sideways.

A long time ago, one of her boyfriends had taken her to an amusement park and persuaded her to buy a ticket for the bumper-car rink. After that, she could never understand why anyone thought it was fun to sit in the scaled-down cars and deliberately try to collide with the other drivers.

But now the satisfying crunch of metal against metal was all she could think about, and she floored the gas, ramming her tormentor again and again and again . . .

Blood pouring out of a cut on his forehead, the driver of the Toyota struggled to regain control as Sarah single-mindedly kept up the assault. He gunned his car in reverse and sent her Camaro spinning backward, colliding into a garbage truck.

Sarah was pitched forward, and her head smashed

against the windshield. Her piercing scream was accompanied by the sickening sound of crumpling steel.

Outside Sarah's hospital room, Katheryn conferred briefly with a police officer who pointed down the hall to a man, his arm wrapped in a bandage, being interviewed by another police officer.

Deborah, the same nurse who had been on duty the night of Sarah's rape, came out of Sarah's room. She recognized Katheryn and nodded. "You can go in, but make it fast. I want to give her a shot."

Katheryn tiptoed inside. Sarah was lying flat on her back, staring fixedly at the blank television set. She had a large bandage on her forehead, an eye that was turning all kinds of colors, and a deep gash that ran from her cheekbone to her mouth.

"What happened?" Katheryn asked quietly.

"'Wanna play some pinball?' That's what he said: 'You wanna play some pinball?'" Sarah spoke so softly that Katheryn could hardly make out her words.

"What? You're not making any sense. Why did you—"

Her voice low and flat, Sarah said, "He figures I'm a piece of shit—everybody figures I'm a piece of shit. Why not? That's what you told everybody. I never got to tell anybody anything. You did all my talking for me."

Sarah went on in the same ominous monotone. "I don't get it. You were supposed to be on my side. You told me you were on my side. Why did you stick it to me? How come you did that? I never did anything bad to you."

After that, she had nothing left to say. She turned her head away and closed her eyes.

Katheryn, so rarely at a loss for words, was speechless in the face of Sarah's calmly voiced accusations. For the truth was that she *had* failed Sarah Tobias. And she knew it.

She had made Sarah a promise—that she would defend her rights—and she had broken that promise. She had betrayed her. Certainly she was not responsible for the incident with Cliff Albrecht. But she couldn't help but feel that certain choices she had made—whether due to personal prejudice or expediency—had indirectly contributed to setting the stage for that incident.

And the sight of Sarah, lying injured and in pain, quietly reminding her of that promise, was far more devastating than Sarah's shrieking and cursing at her dinner party.

She left Sarah's room feeling terribly ashamed of herself. At the other end of the hall, Cliff Albrecht was walking toward the exit. She caught up with him outside, in the hospital parking lot.

"Mr. Albrecht?" she called.

He glanced at her and said, "What do you want?"

"I understand you were in an accident. I wanted to ask you what happened."

"It was her fuckin' fault, not mine," Albrecht said. He looked at her suspiciously. "Are you a friend of hers or something?"

Katheryn smiled politely. "We're professionally connected. What exactly happened?"

"She fuckin' rammed into my car. I was minding my own business, and she drove her car into me." He pointed to the bandage, which covered his arm from his shoulder to his elbow.

Just below the elbow, on the inside of his forearm, was a tattoo of a scorpion.

"Do you know why?" asked Katheryn, her mind registering the tattoo.

"How the fuck do I know why she rammed me? She's nuts!"

"Do you know her?"

"No," he said sourly. "I don't know her. She's a whore. Last time I saw her, she was doing a sex show."

Katheryn struggled to keep the emotion from her face. "You were there?"

"Fuckin' A," he spat.

"And you watched?"

Albrecht nodded vigorously. "You're fuckin' A right I watched. She puts on a great show."

"I thought she was raped," said Katheryn, sounding puzzled.

"Raped?" Albrecht hooted derisively. "She fucked a bar full of guys and then blamed them for it."

Albrecht's wife pulled up in his badly dented Toyota.

"Move over," he ordered her.

He had one last thought for Katheryn. "Listen, lady, she loved it. She had an audience, and she did the show of her fuckin' life."

Mrs. Albrecht said timidly, "Are you sure you should drive with—"

"Move over," he growled. He lowered his voice and leered at Katheryn. "You tell her from me, any time she wants to put on another show, I'll be right there to cheer her the fuck on."

Too stunned to speak, Katheryn watched him get into his car and roar away. She slammed her fist down on the hood of the car next to her and silently sent him a message: *Watch out, Mr. Albrecht.*

Because from now on Cliff Albrecht wouldn't have much to cheer about. Katheryn Murphy intended to go after him with every weapon she had. She would make him regret that he had ever stood by and cheered Sarah's "show." She had the power to make it up to Sarah Tobias. And no matter what it took, she was going to make damned sure she made full use of that power.

CHAPTER ELEVEN

LATE THAT EVENING, KATHERYN WENT BACK TO the office and sat down at her desk.

Her tape recorder was buried beneath her papers and books. She retrieved it and inserted the tape of the call for help that had been made to the county sheriff's office the night of the rape.

"Listen, there's a girl in trouble," the man said in a hurried, strained voice. "There's an assault going on, a rape, okay? . . . three . . . four . . . I don't know, there's a crowd . . ."

Katheryn hit stop, rewound the tape, then listened to it over and over again. ". . . three . . . four . . . I don't know, there's a crowd . . ."

She took out Sarah's file and carefully reread her notes from that night.

The line leaped out at her: "A whole bunch—yelled and clapped."

Flipping forward several pages to her interview

with Sarah's friend Sally, she found the other line she had been looking for: "Some guys blocked view . . . real rowdy."

There it was. Right there in front of her nose.

Fueled with coffee and anger, Katheryn worked through the night, researching the criminal codes for legal precedent, carefully constructing her new case. By dawn she was too excited to feel her fatigue.

She had hit upon the solution that would belatedly afford Sarah Tobias her day in court.

As soon as the corner coffee shop opened, she had them send up fresh coffee and a fried egg sandwich. When Al poked his head in the door to say good morning, she was ready. Not bothering to explain, she dragged him down to Paul's office and stuck her legal pad under Paul's nose.

"I'd like you to take a look at this," she said. "I've rethought the Sarah Tobias case."

At the top of the page she had written in large letters: CRIMINAL SOLICITATION.

Paul frowned. "Dammit, Katheryn," he sighed, wondering what had gotten into her. "Criminal solicitation simply doesn't apply. It's not the intent of the statute."

Katheryn flipped open a law book to the page she had marked. "Listen again," she told Paul and Al. "A person is guilty of criminal solicitation if he commands, induces, entreats, or otherwise attempts to persuade another person to commit a felony."

"You can read it to me till you're blue in the face. I'm not going to let you prosecute a bunch of spectators," Paul retorted.

"Goddammit, Paul, they're not spectators," Katheryn said heatedly. "They solicited the rape."

Al raised a skeptical eyebrow. "Do you really want to go into court and ask a jury to lock up a bunch of people for clapping and cheering?"

"Clapping, cheering, pushing, goading—getting the rape going and keeping it going. I want to try this case."

"If you lose, you look like an incompetent. If you win, you look like a vengeful bitch," Paul assured her. "Either way, you hurt yourself and you hurt this office." His tone softened. "Drop it. You've got more important things to do."

She shook her head vigorously. "No, I haven't."

"What? You haven't got more important things to do than go to trial with a sure loser? What the hell has gotten into you?"

"We owe her," Katheryn said quietly.

"Owe her what? We put the rapists away."

"*I* owe her."

His face red with anger, Paul shouted, "I see! You want to spend my money to put a bunch of spectators on trial—a trial you'll lose—because you owe her. No. You don't get to use this office to pay your debts, Katheryn. No!"

Katheryn spoke with steely determination. "Paul, I am going to try this case, and you're not going to stop me."

"I'm not? Katheryn, you're an ace, and you've got a great future. Don't put it in jeopardy. Don't make me fire you."

"Go ahead," she said calmly. "My first case will be

a multimillion-dollar civil suit against the rapists, the solicitors, the bar—*and* the state. And I will show that Sarah Tobias wound up in a hospital because this office sold her out. I will subpoena your records and put you on the stand and cross-examine you on every sleazy plea bargain this office has ever made."

A muscle twitched in Paul's jaw. "Al, I want all of Miss Murphy's cases reassigned." He stood up and pointed a finger at Katheryn. "Go try your case. And have a good time, because win or lose, you're through."

Two days later, after Sarah had been released from the hospital, Katheryn drove over to her trailer to talk to her.

Loud music greeted her as soon as she got out of her car. She banged on the door until Sarah appeared, wearing a neck brace.

"Hello, Sarah. May I come in? I'd like to talk to you."

"We got nothin' to talk about," Sarah snapped.

"Yes, we—"

The door slammed shut.

Katheryn knocked again, then twisted the doorknob. It was unlocked, and she stepped inside.

Sarah was lying on the bed. "Get out!" she shouted above the music.

"Can you lower that, please?" said Katheryn. Sarah didn't move, so Katheryn went over to the stereo and lowered the volume. "Sarah, I have to talk to you," she said.

"Get out of my way!" Sarah jumped up and tried to

step around Katheryn to get at the stereo, but Katheryn grabbed her arm. "Let me go!" Sarah protested angrily.

"Will you listen to me?"

"Let me go!" she yelled.

After Katheryn dropped her hand, Sarah said sullenly, "I'm listening."

"Sarah," Katheryn admitted slowly, "I made a mistake. Before I agreed to the deal, I should have offered you the choice of going to trial and testifying. I can offer it to you now."

Sarah stared at her suspiciously, as if Katheryn were babbling at her in a foreign language that she couldn't comprehend.

"Do you understand me?" Katheryn went on. "I've found a way for you to go into court and testify that you were raped."

"The case is over," Sarah said flatly.

"The *rape* case is over."

"You made sure of that."

Katheryn knew she deserved the rebuke. She accepted it without comment. "I want to prosecute the others—the ones who cheered and clapped. The ones who made it happen."

"So you can make another deal?" Sarah taunted her.

"I'm not going to make another deal," Katheryn promised. "Sarah, if I prosecute the others the rapists will stay inside for the whole five years—and the rape will go on record. The deal won't matter because the rape will go on record."

Sarah didn't trust Katheryn's total about-face, although the offer certainly was tempting. Especially now, when she could hardly move without the damn neck brace getting in her way.

And all she could think about was Cliff Albrecht's leering smile and his mocking cry: "You wanna play some pinball?" She knew she would be haunted by those words for the rest of her life.

But why was Katheryn Murphy suddenly so ready to help her? Katheryn didn't like her. She could sense that. She wasn't even sure Katheryn believed her story.

She went over to the refrigerator and took out two cans of soda. Let her know that Sarah Tobias wasn't the pothead lush Miss Deputy D.A. had made her out to be.

She popped open the tabs, stuck straws inside, and handed one to Katheryn.

"Thank you," said Katheryn.

"You really gonna do it?" Sarah asked warily.

"Only if you help. I need you to testify."

"I get to tell my story?"

"Yes." Katheryn could feel Sarah relishing the prospect of publicly pointing an accusing finger at Cliff Albrecht and the others. *Do it, Sarah,* she silently urged her. *Say yes.*

Sarah nodded grudgingly.

Katheryn smiled her thanks. As she turned to go, she noticed that the trailer looked different. Less cluttered. A lot fewer books and records. The guitar and amplifier she had noticed last time were gone now. A couple of the posters were missing.

"Are you by yourself now?" she asked.

"Yeah, I kicked him out. Then, while I was laid up, he came back to get his stuff." Sarah laughed bitterly. "You know, like, what's his is his, and what's mine is his. At least he left me the stereo."

Sarah talked tough, but Katheryn could see that she was hurting badly. She felt a swell of sympathy for her. "Is there anything I can do?" she offered.

For a brief moment, Sarah was tempted to say, "Yes, stay and talk to me. I feel terrible. I need a friend."

But she had learned early that strangers were not to be trusted. Their offers all too often came with long strings attached. Then her pride got the better of her, and the moment to reach out was gone.

Still, there was something Katheryn could do for her.

"Yeah," she said slowly.

"What?" Katheryn said. "Tell me."

Sarah smiled wanly. "No deals."

"No," Katheryn promised. "No deals."

There was no answer when Katheryn rang the bell at Sally Frazer's house. But a VW was parked in the driveway, so Katheryn walked around to the back of the house. A wall of wet sheets was hanging from the clothesline, and a pair of legs was visible below the sheets.

"Sally?" Katheryn said. "It's Katheryn Murphy. I need your help again."

Sally peered at her from between the sheets. "I thought it was all over."

"I'm going to prosecute the ones who cheered it

on," Katheryn explained. She grabbed a handful of clothespins from the laundry basket and handed a couple to Sally.

"I told you, I don't know anyone," Sally said nervously, nodding her thanks.

"Let's come back to that," Katheryn said. Referring to her notepad, she quoted Sally's words back to her. "Now . . . 'real rowdy' . . . 'yelling and clapping.' Do you remember what they were yelling?"

"Y'know." Sally grimaced. "'Show us your tits,' 'take it off,' stupid shit like that."

"That's all?"

"I don't know," she said, busying herself again with the laundry. "'Hold her down' . . . 'pussy'—something about pussy—it was kind of a . . . a chant about pussy. Other stuff, too. Really raw, you know what I'm sayin'?"

Her eyes were full of pain, remembering.

"Did you know they were yelling about Sarah?" Katheryn asked, scribbling down Sally's words.

"I just thought they were being jerks. I didn't know anything bad was going on. I mean, if I'd thought she really needed help, I woulda done something. Honest—she's my friend."

"So you knew they were yelling about her?"

"Shit, yeah," Sally admitted, her pale cheeks flaming red with shame. "But these guys aren't the kind of guys you mess with, you know what I'm sayin'?"

Katheryn closed her notebook. "I'd like you to see if you could pick any of them out of a lineup."

"Yeah," Sally said with obvious reluctance. "I guess I could do that."

"And then I'd like you to testify to what you heard them yell."

Sally stared at her as if she had lost her mind. "You mean, like, in court?"

"Yes."

"Jesus! They're gonna be right there, aren't they?"

"Yes."

"Jesus!"

"Let's make a date for you to come in and go over it with me," Katheryn said quickly, before Sally lost her nerve.

Sally stared at the ground. "I don't know."

"Sally," Katheryn said quietly, "she's your friend."

A long pause, then Sally met her gaze. "What the hell . . . okay."

"Thank you," said Katheryn. And silently cheered, *All right!*

Sally gave Katheryn the names of the men she remembered screaming and cheering at the Mill. Dunc rounded up the three of them and had them brought in. It took Sally all of five minutes to identify Cliff Albrecht, Stuart Holloway, and Matt Haines.

Katheryn left the police station feeling, for the first time in a long time, as if she had earned her salary.

On the way to her car, she was intercepted by a young, vaguely familiar woman who appeared to be very agitated.

"Miss Murphy?" the woman stammered, "I'm Barbara Albrecht, Cliff's wife."

Now Katheryn remembered—the woman sitting in

the driver's seat of Cliff's car that day at the hospital. "How do you do," she said.

Barbara Albrecht looked young and easily intimidated. She had frightened brown doe's eyes, and she blinked rapidly as she spoke. Accosting strangers—especially deputy district attorneys—was obviously not something she did often or easily.

In a timid, shaky voice, she asked, "Why is my husband under arrest?"

"He's charged with a crime," said Katheryn, wondering what could have attracted this sweet-faced woman to a coarse, vulgar bully like Cliff Albrecht.

"I don't get it," Mrs. Albrecht said. "He didn't rape anyone, he didn't do anything. He was having a drink with his friends. That's not a crime. What did he do?"

She sounded genuinely puzzled as she struggled to hold back the tears in her eyes.

"Mrs. Albrecht," explained Katheryn, "he'll be formally accused of criminal solicitation—encouraging other people to commit a felony."

"What does that mean?"

"I'm afraid I can't discuss that with you, Mrs. Albrecht. You should take it up with his lawyer."

Hoping the woman would get the message, Katheryn turned away and walked toward her car.

But Barbara Albrecht was desperate. Cliff sometimes drank too much, and he could get tough and mean with her. But he was the only husband she had.

She hurried to catch up with Katheryn and said in a pleading voice, "It's the girl's fault. Everybody knows what she did. And then she tried to run him down. Why don't you arrest *her?*"

Katheryn understood the woman's position, but her persistence was annoying.

"If your husband wants to swear out a complaint, the district attorney's office will act on it," she said coldly. "Now, excuse me, Mrs. Albrecht, I'm late for an appointment."

Normally shy and passive, Barbara Albrecht surprised even herself as she grabbed Katheryn's arm and forced her to stop. Almost whimpering, she said, "All he was doing was having a drink with his friends. You can't put him in prison for that. You *can't!*"

Katheryn pulled herself free. "Mrs. Albrecht," she said flatly, "I'm sorry, but you're talking to the wrong person. I'm prosecuting your husband. You should be talking to *his* lawyer."

She briskly nodded good-bye and walked away. Absorbed in her own thoughts, she didn't even hear Barbara Albrecht's mournful cry.

"All he was doing was having a drink with his friends."

CHAPTER TWELVE

NEITHER SARAH NOR SALLY HAD EVER BEEN IN the Criminal Courts building before. Sally was feeling intimidated by the lawyers with their three-piece suits and briefcases who rode up in the elevator with them. But the lawyers didn't bother Sarah. She had a right to be there, and she was going to go up against those lawyers defending the Mill guys, and she was going to *win.*

With Sally trailing a step behind her, Sarah announced herself and Sally to the receptionist, who pointed them down the corridor to the D.A.'s suite. The door to Katheryn's office was half open. Sarah knocked once and walked in.

Katheryn was on the phone with Ben Wainwright, Cliff Albrecht's lawyer. She glanced up, waved at the two women, and put up a finger to signal that she would be just another moment.

Sarah sat down in one of the chairs in front of

Katheryn's desk and motioned to Sally to do likewise.

"There's no purpose in a meeting, Ben," Katheryn said firmly, "because I'm taking it to trial. Good luck to you, too." She chuckled before she hung up.

"Hi. Thank you for coming, Sally. Sarah, you didn't need to come," she said gently.

"I didn't mind." Sarah shrugged, settling herself into the chair. "I wanted to say hello, see how it was going."

Katheryn was touched that Sarah had taken the time to come downtown to see her. Maybe it was her way of saying she had forgiven Katheryn for the plea bargain and that she trusted her to do a good job with her case.

But Katheryn had no intention of allowing her to participate in the meeting with Sally. She wanted to hear Sally's side of the story without any prompting or the pressure of her friend sitting next to her, listening to every word.

So she said, "Well, could you wait outside? Actually, there's a coffee shop around the corner."

Sarah got the hint, and she didn't like it. "Uh, sure," she said, not bothering to hide her annoyance. "I'll wait outside."

She stalked out and plopped herself down on a chair in the hall next to Katheryn's office. Through the open door, she could hear Katheryn say, "Sally, let's begin with when Sarah came into the Mill. Was she drinking a lot?"

She leaned over to hear Sally's answer, but just then Katheryn stuck her head out of the room, smiled, and shut the door. There was nothing for Sarah to do but put on her Walkman and try to relax.

On the other side of the door, Sally picked nervously at her nails and thought back to that Saturday night. "Well," she said, "I wasn't counting—maybe she had two drinks, maybe three. She wasn't drunk or anything. I've seen her drink a lot more than that. Loose, you know?" She glanced questioningly at Katheryn, who nodded at her to continue. "I mean, she needed to get loose, you know, 'cause she just had this big fight with Larry."

"The man she lives with?"

"Yeah, her old man. And she goes, 'I'm so pissed at him!' 'cause she's sure he's running around on her."

"You mean sleeping with somebody else?"

"Right. Which I bet he is. So these two fraternity guys were there, and Sarah looks at one of them—Bob—and she goes, 'He's cute, who's he?' So we start jokin' around and—"

"What do you mean, 'joking around'?"

Sally looked uncomfortable. "You know, girl stuff, like what would be the best way to get back at him, like she should take this guy home and do it right in front of Larry."

An image was beginning to form in Katheryn's mind that she didn't much like. "You said she should take Bob home?" she asked.

"No, no, she said it," Sally said, her stomach churning again. She could see from the look on Katheryn's face that she was getting the wrong idea.

"She was just joking around. She didn't mean it,"

Sally assured Katheryn. "She had a couple of drinks and . . . she didn't mean it."

The interview went downhill from there. The more Katheryn probed, the more Sally squirmed as she gave her version of what had gone on that night. After twenty minutes of questioning, too distressed to sit still, Katheryn stood up and began to pace her office.

The foundation on which she had planned to build her case was crumbling before her, and she didn't have a clue to how she could salvage it. Sally's testimony was as damning to Sarah as the defense attorneys could have hoped for—and she, Katheryn, had all but pointed Sally in their direction.

Not that it mattered anymore, but Paul would have a good time with this, too. She could just see him rubbing his hands with gleeful vindication as he chuckled knowingly about women who thought they could win cases with cobwebs and fairy dust.

She was furious with Sarah on whose behalf she had taken this risk. She had put herself on the line. Now it was Katheryn's turn to feel betrayed.

Eventually there were no questions left to ask. She had gotten what she could from Sally. Katheryn thanked her for her cooperation and promised to be in touch.

Sally knew the interview had gone badly, but she had had no choice. For if she lied to Katheryn, she would have to tell the same lies in court, which of course she couldn't do. She hated to think how angry Sarah would be with her, though Sally had tried to explain that it hadn't happened the way it seemed. No matter what Sarah had said, she wasn't looking to get laid, and those men had no right to say she had been asking for it.

But she couldn't face Sarah just now, so she bolted out of Katheryn's office, told Sarah she would call her later, and rushed off toward the elevators.

Sarah needed only one look at Katheryn's face to know something was up.

"What's the matter?" she asked worriedly.

"Let's not talk about it here," Katheryn said, barely controlling herself.

"Hey, my best friend just ran away like a thief. What's going on?" Sarah demanded.

Katheryn spoke quietly, but the sharp edge of anger in her voice was unmistakable. "I warned you—don't keep secrets from me."

"I haven't kept—"

"Sally told me what you said when you saw Bob. Do you remember? Do you, Sarah?" Katheryn clenched her fists by her side. It was all she could do not to grab Sarah by the arms and shake her into understanding the gravity of the situation.

Sarah remembered exactly what she had said. "'I'd like to take that guy home and fuck his brains out right in front of Larry.' So what?" she asked defiantly. "It was a joke. Lighten up."

"So what?" Katheryn repeated. "So she can't be a witness for you, that's so what. In fact, when the defense finds her—and they will—she'll be a witness for them, and she'll kill you. Now, what other surprises do you have waiting for me?"

Sarah stared at her in shock and anger. "None!" she shouted. "None!"

After all her fine talk about justice and vindication, Katheryn had painted her own distorted picture that featured Sarah as the guilty one. She was no different from Cliff Albrecht, Sarah thought bitterly. In fact, she was worse, because she pretended to listen and to care. At least with Albrecht there were no tricks. She knew where she stood with him.

Sarah grabbed her bag and stormed down the corridor without another word.

Katheryn stared after her, wondering whether Sarah was truly that stupid or just terribly naive. Or was it she, who prided herself on her intellect and her street smarts, who was the stupid one?

What was going on with this case? she wearily asked herself. Time and again she was losing her cool, not asking all the right questions, not seeing all that was there to be seen.

Thoroughly discouraged and exhausted, she checked her watch and decided to call it a day before she uncovered any other piece of evidence custom-designed to skewer Sarah Tobias and her case. She packed her briefcase, turned off the lights, and left the building.

Halfway to her car, she saw Dunc waving at her from across the street.

He trotted over and said, "Hey! How's it going?"

"It isn't," she said glumly.

"Oh," Dunc scratched his bald head. "Well, I don't suppose this is going to help."

She knew she shouldn't ask, but she did. "What?"

Dunc pursed his lips. "Polito's skipped."

"Oh no!" The last thing she wanted to hear at the end of this day. "Are you sure?"

"Look," Dunc said sympathetically, "I'm not working on your case anymore, but I thought I'd lean on Polito a little on my own time. He's definitely gone—I checked it out."

"Shit."

"Sorry. How about you? Any luck with the video player?"

"No. But I'm going to try Jesse one more time. Do you want to come along?" she asked hopefully.

"I think I'll pass." Dunc grinned.

Dunc was a good friend, someone she trusted. She said, "Dunc, do you think I'm crazy for pushing this? Do you agree with Paul?"

"Fuck Paul," Dunc replied in his blunt way. "I've got a firebombing at an after-hours joint, a gang of fourteen-year-olds with an arsenal in their lockers, and enough drug dealers to keep me busy until I collect my pension. You think I got time to worry about infighting at the D.A.'s office?"

"In other words, you think I'm right?"

"In other words, I think you and I have made a lot of cases together, and you always had guts. Now you're probably gonna lose this one, but you're a big girl, and we've lost cases before, so—"

"We? I thought you weren't working on this anymore."

"I'm not." He winked. "But I'll let you know as

soon as I find the guy that made that call. See ya," he said with a cheerful wave.

"See ya," said Katheryn, feeling a whole lot better than she had ten minutes earlier.

She got into her car, still preoccupied with all the pieces that were continuously shifting around and changing the shape of this puzzling case. The video game player, she mused. There had to be some way . . .

Her thoughts were interrupted when Sarah tapped on her window, signaling her to roll it down.

"Sorry," she said softly. Then she walked away without another word.

Katheryn smiled wryly. Maybe she could score in the final quarter after all.

CHAPTER THIRTEEN

KATHERYN HAD NEITHER SEEN NOR HEARD FROM Connie since she had moved into her own apartment. A couple of times she had tried calling her, but there was never any answer. Probably Connie was trying to keep busy. Katheryn knew how much she hated being alone.

After the disastrous meeting with Sally, Katheryn felt too distracted to work on any of the files she had brought home with her. On an impulse, she decided to drop by and surprise Connie. The visit would do them both good.

She picked out some records she thought Connie might like and stopped by the bakery for treats. Connie was a chocolate doughnut freak. Katheryn bought half a dozen and threw in four large chocolate chip cookies for good measure.

Connie's apartment was on the first floor of a three-story house in one of the older sections of the city. It lacked the amenities of Katheryn's building—no doorman, no mirrored lobby, no laundry room conveniently located on each floor. But it had large bay windows, a fireplace, and a backyard with lots of bushes and a flower garden.

A nice, cozy place, Katheryn had thought when she and Connie had gone to look at it.

She knocked on the door. No answer. She tried the buzzer. Still no answer. Maybe this had been a dumb idea. She should have called ahead to make sure Connie was at home. She pressed the buzzer one last time and finally got a response.

"Who is it?" Connie said, her voice muffled.

"It's me, Katheryn."

"Katheryn?"

"Yeah. I came to see your place."

A few seconds later Connie opened the door. She was dressed in one of her satin robes, and her face was perfectly made up. Her hair was loose and falling all over her face and shoulders, and in her left hand was a lit cigarette.

"You have a great sense of timing," she told Katheryn.

Katheryn could have kicked herself. "Sorry," she said self-consciously. "Are you busy?"

"Yeah . . ."

"Company?" asked Katheryn, knowing it was none of her business.

"Yeah." Connie nodded, waving away the cigarette smoke.

"Okay. Maybe some other time then," Katheryn

said lightly, pretending to be less disappointed than she was.

"Maybe, but call first, okay?"

"Sure."

Walking toward her car, Katheryn laughed scornfully at herself for giving in to sisterly sentiment. So much for her concern that her sister might be lonely. That had never been Connie's problem. Katheryn's big sister was one person who knew how to go out and find herself some fun.

Since she was already headed in the direction of the Mill, and since she had nothing better to do at home than work, Katheryn decided now was as good a time as any to pay another call on Jesse. Maybe he could help her out with the identity of the man who had called the sheriff's office.

Questions about the so-called Good Samaritan nagged at her. With all the publicity the case was getting, why hadn't he come forward? He had cared enough to make the call, so what was stopping him now? Unless, perhaps, he had a reason to hold back: a criminal record . . . or maybe he was a friend of one of the defendants.

Something Sally had said teased at her: "These two fraternity guys were there . . ."

Maybe that was it. Maybe Bob Joiner had brought along a friend that night. But Bob Joiner must have dozens of frat brothers, none of whom had admitted to being present at the Mill. Short of questioning each and every one of them, she had no way of finding the one guy she needed to talk to.

If there were a missing frat boy, could he be the same kid Jesse had mentioned to Dunc—the one Jesse hadn't seen before—the one who had been playing video games all night?

She would have to jog Jesse's memory a little bit for a description of the video guy. Because otherwise, what with Arthur Polito having skipped town and Sally turning out to be a time bomb of damaging testimony, she was about to have no case whatsoever.

It would be a hell of a way to end her career at the district attorney's office, she thought ruefully. Not to mention Ted Millbank's reaction when the news of her royal screw-up got around town.

Oh God, she thought, for the hundredth time. *Why couldn't Sarah Tobias have stayed home that night, worked it out with her boyfriend, and gotten herself laid instead of raped?*

She pulled into the Mill parking lot and followed a crew of what appeared to be construction workers into the bar, which was packed with happy-hour drinkers. The place was jumping—music blaring, customers laughing and shouting above the noise of the TV, the pinball machines and video games screeching from the other room.

The man tending bar told her that Jesse didn't come on for another half-hour, but "Hey, I like to serve a pretty face. What's your pleasure?"

Katheryn ordered a beer and wandered into the game room. For a minute or two she stood watching the scene. A couple was dancing very close in the middle of the room, oblivious to the fast beat of the music.

A group of men dressed in work clothes was gathered around the pinball machines, jostling for a chance at the machines, trading good-natured gibes. The garishly lit video games were also pulling in their share of customers.

She stared curiously at the players, wondering whether any of them had been present that night. Absorbed in her thoughts, she didn't realize at first that a bunch of the men were very openly checking her out. When she returned their stares, one of them winked and licked his lips suggestively. Then he turned to his pals and made a crack that had them laughing boisterously and slapping each other on the back.

Ignore them, she told herself. *They're stupid, harmless jerks.*

As harmless as the men who had gang-raped Sarah Tobias?

She gazed at the pinball machine, now silent, on which the rape had taken place, and she tried to imagine herself there, in Sarah's place, struggling to get free, squirming against the cold, hard glass and metal surface of the machine, unable to cry out for help, her ears ringing with the excited cheers of the onlookers.

Dammit, it didn't matter whether Sarah had smoked a joint and drunk a couple of beers, whether she had joked with Sally about getting back at Larry by sleeping with another man. It didn't even matter whether she had flirted with one of the other customers.

She hadn't deserved what had come to her.

Bastards, Katheryn swore silently, and she glanced again at the bank of video games, looking for answers. And then suddenly she found what she and Dunc had missed before. At the top of each screen was an electronic scroll that listed the players and their best scores. She quickly scanned one game after another, until finally one line leaped out at her.

"'Enduro Racer'—4/18/87—Philip."

April 18, the night of Sarah's rape.

Who was Philip? Bob Joiner's fraternity brother? The voice on the telephone tape? Or just an innocent guy who'd come into the Mill for a few beers?

Her apartment was a mess, but Katheryn didn't care. She sat down at her dining-room table with her law books, legal pad, tape recorder, tape cassettess, and container of takeout food, her dinner. With one eye on the television, she reread Sarah Tobias's file, making neat little check marks in the margin where appropriate. But her attention was suddenly caught by the anchorman's statement that coming up was a Channel 3 editorial on recent actions taken by the district attorney's office.

A spokeswoman for the station read from a prepared statement: "The other night this station broadcast an editorial applauding Assistant District Attorney Katheryn Murphy for bringing charges in a new case linked to the assault at the Mill. We disagree with that editorial. We don't think the charges should have been brought. We believe that Ms. Murphy is muddling moral and legal issues and using the law—the wrong law—to impose her moral standards on the rest of us. If there's one thing we've all learned, it's that you cannot legislate morality."

"Fuck you," Katheryn told the screen.

The phone rang. Startled, she picked it up and said, "Hello?"

"Hi, it's David."

"It's nice to hear from you finally," Katheryn said with a hint of sarcasm. "Were you that upset when I asked you to leave?"

"No. Actually, I am upset, but not about that," David stammered. "Well, I'm not upset, really, but Ted Millbank is very uncomfortable with what you're doing . . . that trial business."

"I'm sorry to hear that," she said tersely.

"I mean," he went on, picking his words cautiously, "very uncomfortable. He wanted to know if it's gone too far for you to . . . to stop it."

"Yes, it has gone too far," Katheryn calmly assured him, disliking David's question and the strange way he was talking to her.

"He doesn't really understand why it's so important. After all, she's really just a slutty little waitress. She's hardly worth the bother." He laughed nervously, waiting for her to bail him out of the hole.

"She is not a slutty little waitress, and she *is* worth the bother," Katheryn replied as calmly as she could manage.

"Ted doesn't think so."

Ted can go to hell, Katheryn thought. Aloud she said, "And I take it you agree with him?"

There was a long pause, then, "Actually, I think I do."

"And?"

He cleared his throat. "Ted feels that if you follow it through . . . you might not be quite the type of attorney who would fit in at the firm. He feels that quite strongly."

"Do you feel that, David?"

"Well, it is a very prestigious firm—"

She couldn't stand to hear another word. "Goodbye, David," she said and slammed down the receiver.

On television a game-show host was smiling at her, describing the prizes to be won on that evening's program. "Fuck you, too," she said and snapped off the set.

Ted Millbank and David had more education than the men who hung out at the Mill. They worked with their heads instead of their hands, and they made more money. And they had a veneer of polish and sophistication that the others lacked.

But at heart, how different were they, really, from Sarah's assailants? They looked at her, and they, too, just saw a "slutty little waitress."

In their eyes, Katheryn was one of them, all because she dressed and spoke and behaved a certain way. But she had deliberately taught herself to fit in. She had worked hard at it, just as she had worked hard to become a top-notch lawyer.

She had even begun to think like them.

Did that make her any better than Sarah? Any less vulnerable to rape? Any worthier of "bother"?

Difficult questions to answer. Questions that could

wait until later, after she had won the case for Sarah. And she would wait to think about David and the kind of man he was, until she had the time to feel her pain.

But now she had work to do.

She searched through the pile of papers for the fraternity "lookbook," an alphabetical listing of all the brothers along with a small photograph next to each entry. She thumbed through, checking the names:

JOHNSON, WILLIAM
JOINER, ROBERT
JOYCE, PHILIP
Bingo!

The next day, the lookbook in hand, she drove over to the fraternity house and waited impatiently in her car for Philip Joyce. When he finally emerged from the house, she got out of her car and called, "Mr. Joyce?" Then she hurried over to catch him.

"Call me Philip," said the young man, mugging for his friends. The woman looked familiar to him, but he couldn't place her. He thought maybe she was a newspaper reporter who wanted to interview him.

Katheryn moved a step closer and said quietly, "Mr. Joyce, I'm Katheryn Murphy. I'd like to talk to you about the night of April eighteenth—the night of the rape at the Mill."

"I don't know anything about it," he quickly blurted.

"Yes you do, Mr. Joyce. Why don't we move over here?" she said, sure that he was lying. She gently took his arm and led him over to a bench on the lawn.

Philip waved at his friends. "I'll catch up with you guys later."

Nervously wiping the palms of his hands on his pants, he tried to remember where he had heard Katheryn Murphy's name before. Then it came to him—they had mentioned her on television. She was the deputy D.A. for Sarah Tobias's case.

He had started worrying again ever since he had heard that Katheryn Murphy had arrested the men from the Mill who had been cheering and shouting while Sarah Tobias was being raped. He remembered those men all too well. He couldn't get out of his mind the image of them screaming obscenities and applauding wildly.

Had she come to arrest him? he suddenly wondered. But that was crazy. All she wanted was to talk to him. He hadn't done anything. He just happened to have been in the wrong place at the wrong time. A witness—who hadn't come forward. But that wasn't a crime . . . or was it?

Then he noticed that Katheryn Murphy had placed a tape recorder next to her on the bench. He hated the way he sounded on tape, so stilted and nervous. What if he stood up now and said, "Sorry, I don't have anything to say to you," and walked away? She couldn't force him to answer her questions.

It was all because of Bob that he had been there—and it was all because of Bob that he was scared to speak up.

Katheryn pressed the RECORD button and smiled to

try to get him to relax. "Mr. Joyce," she began, "you were there—your name is listed on the Enduro machine—and I'm calling you as a witness."

The damn video game! He remembered all of a sudden seeing his name there. He had rung up a good score that night, and he was feeling pretty good, like a real hotshot. At least until the party had gotten dirty.

"What do you want with me?" he said unhappily. "You got the ones who did it."

"I'm prosecuting the others—the ones who cheered them on."

"I didn't see a thing," he said defensively.

"Yes you did. Mr. Joyce, you were in the room all night. You saw everything," said Katheryn, watching him closely.

He was hiding something. She was certain of that. Something very painful and hard to admit. He looked like a nice kid, decent, not a smart aleck. She tried to picture him at the Mill, but he didn't fit in there. He was too . . . wholesome.

"The others didn't do anything," he said, shaking his head vigorously from side to side. "They probably didn't know what was going on—it was like a show. Big deal . . . they watched. I bet if you asked a thousand people, nine hundred and ninety-nine would watch. That's no crime!"

"They did more than watch, and that is a crime. Why don't you tell me about it?" she said gently.

Philip shook his head again. There was nothing to tell. Bob was his closest friend, his frat brother.

Katheryn sighed, frustrated by his stubbornness.

"Mr. Joyce, if you don't tell me about it now, you're still going to have to tell me about it on the stand."

"Why? Why?" he demanded, his eyes wide with anguish. "This isn't my business. I don't care about this! You put my best friend in prison—that's all I care about. I don't care about those guys. I don't care about the girl. I don't care about any of it!"

She listened carefully to his impassioned words. He was lying because he was frightened. And his voice, his tone so worried and tense . . .

And then it all clicked into place. She quickly removed the tape and replaced it with the cassette the sheriff's office had given her.

"Yes, you do care, Mr. Joyce," she said. She pressed PLAY, and there he was again, the same voice, sounding strained and desperate, pleading for help.

The look of shock on Philip's face confirmed it for her.

He stared at the machine, dumbfounded. It had never occurred to him that his call had been recorded.

Katheryn reinserted the first tape. She sat back expectantly and said, "Go ahead, Mr. Joyce."

CHAPTER FOURTEEN

WHEN KATHERYN SHOWED UP AT SARAH'S TRAILer at eight o'clock, on the morning Sarah was set to testify in court, Sarah felt like a little kid whose mom thought she needed help picking out her school clothes.

Sarah stuffed another handful of potato chips—her breakfast—into her mouth and washed them down with iced tea before she let Katheryn in. "You said nine," she complained grumpily.

"I woke up early," Katheryn explained. She was wearing a navy-blue suit, a pink silk blouse, and pearls. Not exactly Sarah's taste, but she could tell that Katheryn had paid a whole lot more for the outfit than Sarah earned in a month.

Katheryn stared critically at Sarah's red dress, which had tiny cap sleeves, a wide black patent-leather belt, and a skirt that came just above her knees.

"What do you think?" said Sarah, pirouetting to give Katheryn the full effect.

"It's a bit . . . how can I put it . . .?"

"You said dressy. This is dressy."

She had planned to wear another dress, but this morning, when she put it on, it made her look so fat and ugly that she had immediately grabbed three others out of the closet. And she hated every one of them.

"It's dressy like . . . a party," Katheryn said, choosing her words carefully. She had tried to explain to Sarah how important it was that she make the right impression today in court. And the red polyester party dress was exactly what she had been afraid of. But she had resisted the temptation to suggest that she be the one to choose Sarah's court outfit.

Now Sarah went over to the bed and held up each of the dresses she had flung there earlier.

"They're pretty, but—"

"Tacky?"

"I didn't say that!"

"Maybe they are tacky, but it's better than looking like you're going to your own funeral."

They were off to a bad start, and today Katheryn couldn't afford any temper tantrums or arguments.

"Let's see what we can find," she said, trying to smooth things over. She quickly riffled through the clothes in Sarah's closet.

Sarah had more important things on her mind. "The aspects are okay," she informed her, "but it would really help if I knew all the lawyers' birthdays. You haven't got those, do you?"

"No," Katheryn said, hardly paying any attention to the question. She pulled out a white empire-waisted cotton dress and handed it to Sarah. "Here, try this."

"Aw, come on! That's from my graduation at Sacred Heart." She looked pleadingly at Katheryn, who stood waiting, with one hand on her hip, waiting for Sarah to model the dress.

"Awright," she grumbled, pulling the dress over her head. "But it won't fit. The damn moths have been feeding on it forever. I suppose I have to wear white cotton panties too?"

She examined herself in the full-length mirror on the back of the closet door. "Ugh! I mean, ugh!"

"Perfect," Katheryn declared. "Ready?"

Sarah giggled. "I can't wear this. I look like a damn virgin."

"Move, Sarah," said Katheryn, thinking Sarah was right. The white dress made Sarah look almost sweet and angelic, which was precisely the effect Katheryn wanted.

"Lemme put on my damn shoes, okay?" She grabbed a few more chips and took another swig of iced tea.

Katheryn looked at her suspiciously.

Sarah read her mind. "Iced tea," she said self-righteously. She offered Katheryn the glass. "Taste it."

"Sarah, could you please hurry?" Katheryn said, eyeing the clock in the kitchen. It was already eight fifty-five, and Katheryn was eager to get to court in plenty of time.

"Hey, they won't start without us," Sarah joked.

Katheryn frowned. "Very funny."

Sarah thought her crack was worth at least a smile. "You're even worse than usual," she said. "You got cramps or something?"

"No. Can we please go now?" Katheryn put her hand on the doorknob and tapped her foot impatiently.

"Hey," said Sarah, seeing through Katheryn's act. "I'm scared, too."

"I am *not* scared," Katheryn lied.

She hadn't felt this nervous since her early days in the D.A.'s office, when she had been frightened every time she had to appear before a judge. She was an excellent lawyer, she had been telling herself since dawn, an outstanding lawyer. And she had a strong case, with two key witnesses—Sarah and Philip Joyce—all set to testify.

Nothing was going to happen that she hadn't already been through a thousand times before. This was a case just like any other case she had handled.

And if she could convince herself of that, she could persuade the jury to find the defendants guilty.

Sarah jauntily slung her purse over her shoulder and held the door open. "I'll come through for you," she promised. "You just come through for me."

Philip waited in the visitors' room for Bob to appear on the other side of the thick glass partition. He had never been inside a jail before. There were bars on the windows even on the visitors' side of the partition, and the windows were so dirty that even without the bars not much light would have penetrated the room.

How could Bob take it? Philip wondered. Stuck in a cell day after day, deprived of his freedom, being told what to do when. How could he keep from going crazy, when he couldn't even pick himself up, put on his running shoes, and take off down the road?

Maybe coming to see Bob today hadn't been such a smart idea. But Bob would probably find out right away that Philip had testified. Philip wanted to talk to him before he had to get up in court. He wanted to assure Bob that it was okay, this had to do with the other guys, not him.

He could leave right now, he supposed. He could write Bob a letter and promise to come visit real soon. But that would be the coward's way, and how could he treat his best buddy like that? And then there was Bob, on the other side of the glass, accompanied by one of the guards.

He smiled and motioned to Philip to pick up the telephone so they could talk to each other.

"Hey, Philip," he said cheerfully. "It's great to see you. You must have cut the whole day to come up here."

"No big deal," said Philip, trying to relax. "How are you doing?"

Bob laughed. "I've been better. How's the big, wide, wonderful world?"

"The same. Listen," Philip said, rushing to get it over with, "they're prosecuting the other guys—the ones who were cheering—and they're making me testify, and I figured I better tell you. You got nothing to worry about, but I figured I should tell you."

"Nothing to worry about?" Bob whispered angrily into the phone. "Are you crazy?"

"You're not on trial. It's the other—"

"What are you going to say?"

Philip stammered, "Well . . . wh-what happened."

"And what happened?" Bob asked sternly, like a teacher waiting for the right answer.

Philip gulped. "You know . . . these guys were cheering while you and Danny and Kurt . . . raped her." There—he had said it straight out.

"Who says I raped her? I'm not in here for rape," Bob said darkly.

"Yeah, but that's because—"

"Philip," Bob said, speaking as if to a not very bright child, "you were there. You saw what she did. I didn't rape her. I shouldn't even be here."

Philip looked away, deeply ashamed of his best friend and angry at Bob for putting him in this difficult position.

"Philip, did you see me rape her?" Bob demanded.

"Well . . ."

"You didn't, did you?"

There was a long pause, and then Philip spoke softly into the telephone. "Yeah, Bob, I did."

"Philip, if you say that, you know what happens to me? Instead of letting me out of here in nine months, the parole board will keep me here for five years!"

Bob could see that Philip was wavering. He pressed his advantage. "Philip, you're my friend—you're my best friend. Best friends don't do this. Don't turn into a shit now—not for her. What has she ever done for you, Philip? Tell me that! Go ahead," he challenged Philip. "Tell me!"

"Bob, they're making me do it." Not that that made him any less of a shit.

Bob stared hard at him through the glass. "All they can do is call you. They can't make you say anything. You don't remember, you had too much to drink, you weren't paying attention, you're too confused to get it straight."

"I don't want to lie, Bob."

Bob let fly his best shot. "Do you want to come visit me here for the next five years?"

Philip winced. The arrow had pierced its target.

CHAPTER FIFTEEN

THE NEWSPAPER REPORTERS AND TV CREWS jumped all over Sarah and Katheryn as soon as they were spotted getting out of Katheryn's car. Katheryn kicked herself mentally for forgetting to warn Sarah about not talking to the press. She hoped Sarah wouldn't lose her cool.

"Miss Murphy," called out one of the reporters, "who else are you putting on the stand?"

"No comment," said Katheryn, hurrying Sarah up the steps of the courthouse.

"Is it true that Arthur Polito skipped town?" asked another.

"No comment," she repeated.

A TV reporter stuck a mike in Sarah's face and said, "Is it true your best friend is testifying for the defense?"

Sarah wheeled around, ready to give the guy hell,

but Katheryn grabbed her arm and propelled her forward.

"No," Katheryn said urgently. "No, Sarah."

"Son of a bitch," Sarah muttered.

Katheryn tightened her grip on Sarah's arm and quietly cautioned her, "Sarah, you can't afford to get crazy now."

The reporters surged after them, throwing out questions.

"Miss Murphy, did you make a deal with—"

"No comment."

"Miss Murphy, how can she identify—"

"No comment."

Under her breath, Katheryn said, "Sarah, did you hear me?"

"Miss, how could you see them to identi—"

"Are you deaf, asshole?" Sarah shouted suddenly. "No comment!"

Laughing and scolding her in the same breath, Katheryn yanked Sarah up the last few steps to the courthouse before she could open her mouth and let fly any more juicy remarks. As soon as they were safely inside the lobby, out of sight of the reporters, she shot Sarah a threatening look.

"Well, he *is* an asshole." Sarah defended herself.

Katheryn couldn't argue with that and didn't try. But she was eager to get Sarah out of harm's way. She buttonholed Al, who had been watching out for them, and said, "Al, take Sarah to the waiting section."

Al was about to lead Sarah away, but she hung back, grabbed Katheryn's hand, and gave her a reassuring squeeze. Then she turned and obediently followed Al down the corridor.

Rubbing her fingers, Katheryn stared after Sarah for a moment before she hurried into the courtroom.

It was a full house today. The three defendants—Cliff Albrecht, Stu Holloway, and Matt Haines. Their families and their lawyers—Ben Wainwright, Jane Meyerhoff, and Dan Paulsen. Reporters and sketch artists from all the area papers and TV stations. Curious spectators. The court recorder and officers. The jury that had been selected over the last few days.

Katheryn took her seat at the prosecution table. She glanced around quickly and nodded at Dunc, seated several rows behind her.

"All rise," boomed the court officer as the judge entered the courtroom.

The judge took his place at the bench and banged his gavel. "Are the people ready?"

Katheryn stood up. "The people are ready, Your Honor."

She had done everything she could do to prepare herself and Sarah for this day. Now, as she waited for Sarah to be called to the witness stand, she felt the adrenaline zap through her veins, and all her doubts fell away.

She was about to do what she loved most in the world. She was about to win this case.

As she walked down the aisle to the witness stand, Sarah's heart was pounding so loudly she worried that people would hear and know how frightened she was. She hoped she wasn't about to pass out.

She hadn't expected there to be so many people in the room, and all of them seemed to be staring at her. Then it finally hit her, what Katheryn had been saying all this time. She was about to get up in front of this packed courtroom and describe to them in excruciating detail the humiliating ordeal of her rape.

Mechanically she followed the court officer's instructions to repeat the oath after him. Her eyes glinting with fear, she stared at Katheryn, as if begging her to make it all come out right.

Katheryn approached the witness stand and smiled a message, "Don't worry. We're in this together." Then she positioned herself just to the left of the witness stand, to give the jury a clear, unobstructed view of Sarah.

"Miss Tobias," she began, "on the night of the rape . . ."

Dan Paulsen immediately jumped to his feet. "Objection! These men are not standing trial for rape."

"Your Honor," Katheryn addressed the judge. "It is imperative that the jury know just exactly what was happening to Miss Tobias before, during, and after the rape."

The judge pursed his lips thoughtfully, then said, "Miss Murphy, you may continue your line of questioning, but be brief. Mr. Paulsen is right. This is not a rape trial."

"Thank you, Your Honor." She turned back to Sarah. "Miss Tobias, can you tell us what happened that night at the Mill?"

Sarah gazed at the crowd of people staring at her

expectantly. She was reminded of how scared she had been in high school, when she would have to get up and give oral reports in front of the class. She had hated how they all stared at her, ready to laugh if she said something stupid, if she stumbled over her words. And she had always felt so unprepared for the teacher's questions.

But she wasn't about to chicken out now. No way. She wanted the bastards to pay. And she wanted the rest of them to think twice the next time they were tempted to have themselves some fun.

She leaned into the microphone and began, just as she and Katheryn had rehearsed it. "My boyfriend and I had kind of a fight, so I got in my car and drove to visit my friend Sally at the Mill. I knew she'd be getting off work soon and we could talk."

"She worked there?" Katheryn prompted her.

"Yeah. She's a waitress like me. Anyway, she was on her break, so we sat in a booth and talked, and then this guy, Danny, sent over some drinks, and then he came over. Sally knew him, so we took the drinks and we were just talking. He was funny, you know, he had a line . . ."

"Had you ever seen him before?"

"No. I didn't know anybody but Sally."

"So then what happened?"

Sarah took a sip of water before she continued. "Well, they were playing pinball in the back room, so Danny and I go in and start playing, and I'm playing with him and this other guy, Bob. So I finish my turn and have a little smoke, a little pot, and somebody puts money in the jukebox, and this song I like comes on. So I started to dance, and then Danny starts dancing with me. Close. I mean, tight close. And then . . ." Her voice dropped to a whisper. "He kissed me."

"I'm sorry, Miss Tobias, could you speak up?"

"He kissed me."

"Didn't you try to stop him?"

Sarah shook her head no, and Katheryn motioned for her to speak into the microphone.

She leaned forward, and her words tumbled out. "No. I let him kiss me. I let him kiss me because I figured he was drunk and stoned, you know, and he'd kiss me and leave me alone. But he put his hand under my shirt and grabbed my breast, and when I tried to push him away, he pulled me really close, and he put his hand on my throat—he's a really strong guy—and the next thing I know . . ."

The courtroom was silent, her voice the only sound. They were all listening to her, waiting to hear what had happened next.

"Please go on, Miss Tobias," Katheryn said.

Sarah cleared her throat nervously. "He kept his hand squeezing my throat, and he pushed me down on the pinball machine, and he ripped down my top and pushed his hand up my skirt and pulled down my underpants. He pulled very hard, and . . . and . . ."

She faltered and began to cry.

"Yes?" Katheryn said quietly.

"He . . . he was almost choking me with one hand, and he pulled his pants down with his other hand, I guess, I don't really know when, but a couple of people were shouting for him to 'go for it' and stuff. And I was trying to move, but he was holding me down so hard, and he jammed his hand right up . . ."

Tears were running down her cheeks in streaky, mascara-blackened tracks, and the words stuck in her throat as she fought to catch her breath.

Go on, you can do it, Katheryn told her silently, nodding her support, trying not to let any feelings show on her face.

"He . . . he was kissing me very hard and jamming his hand up my crotch . . . and I could hear them saying, 'Hold her down, hold her down' . . ."

Sarah's piteous sobs echoed through the silent courtroom, but she determinedly continued her grim recitation. "They were cheering and yelling, and this big guy Kurt was holding my arms down, and Danny was inside me, and he had his hand in my mouth, and I shut my eyes and they switched. I heard them saying 'Frat boy' something, 'Go get her, frat boy'—and Bob was inside me, but Kurt was still holding me down, and there was all this shouting and laughing and clapping . . ."

Katheryn was playing a risky game, exposing Sarah's pain for all to see. For the jury to hear and remember. But she had to trust her instincts. One thing she had come to respect about Sarah Tobias—the woman had plenty of grit and determination.

Those qualities showed now as Sarah struggled to get control of herself and went on, still sobbing. "I kept trying to move, but I couldn't, and I wanted to yell, but either they were kissing me or somebody had a hand over my mouth, and they were yelling at Kurt— 'needle dick' or something. They switched again, and Kurt got inside me, and they were yelling, 'Kurt, Kurt, Kurt,' and they were chanting . . ."

She broke down again, but Katheryn said, "Please continue, Miss Tobias. What did they chant?"

Her tremulous voice could hardly be heard, even with the help of the microphone. "Something like 'Poke that pussy' . . . they kept chanting, and Kurt's hand was pressing down hard on my face, and it slipped and I bit it, I bit it and screamed, but there was all this noise . . ."

"The room was full of people cheering this on?"

"Until the music stopped. Then the cheering stopped . . . and I—I kicked him. I kicked him as hard as I could, and I jumped up and ran out. Then this guy picked me up on the road and drove me to the hospital."

Sarah buried her face in her hands. Her shoulders shook convulsively as she let go with great, shuddering sobs that seemed to fill every corner of the hushed courtroom. The spectators, even the merely curious, shifted uncomfortably in their seats and looked away, stricken by Sarah's heartrending testimony.

"No further questions, Your Honor," Katheryn said quietly. She handed Sarah a wad of tissues and gave her a tiny, brief smile of encouragement before she returned to the prosecution table.

A quick, huddled conference took place among the defense attorneys before Ben Wainwright slowly walked over to the witness box. Wainwright, a burly white-haired man, had been hired by Cliff Albrecht. The look of grave concern on his face didn't fool Katheryn. Wainwright was the "good cop" of the team. It didn't bode well for Sarah that they were sending him in first.

Wainwright clasped his hands behind his back and said sympathetically, "Miss Tobias, my name is Ben Wainwright. I realize this isn't easy for you, so I'm going to ask only a handful of questions. Now, you testified that all the men present were strangers to you, and you've also testified that while you were on the pinball machine you mostly kept your eyes shut. Is that right, your eyes were shut?"

"Yes," Sarah said through a blur of tears. "Sometimes."

"Is it fair to say, then," Wainwright asked, sounding as if he greatly regretted having to ask her these questions, "that you can't tell us *who* shouted or *who* applauded?"

"Well, I'm not—"

Wainwright didn't give her a chance to finish. "Might it have been only one person who shouted?"

At the defense table, Paulsen and Meyerhoff exchanged uneasy looks. They had agreed to put up a united front. Was Wainwright about to double-cross them?

"No," Sarah sniffled. "They overlapped."

"At least two, then. Could it have been only two?"

Sarah hesitated, then said, "I don't think so."

Wainwright nodded, as if he were pleased with her

response. "Now, you testified that three men assaulted you, is that right?"

"Yes," she said defiantly.

"Is it possible—just possible—that the only men shouting were among your assaulters?" Wainwright's tone implied that he certainly understood how easy it might have been for Sarah to confuse the voices.

Katheryn immediately saw where he was headed and worried that Sarah would take the bait. But no.

She said, "I don't think so. There were more voices coming from farther away."

Moving closer to the witness box, his voice warm and persuasive, he said, "Miss Tobias, you had had several drinks, you had smoked marijuana, the jukebox was playing, the TV was playing. You were in a room full of noisy pinball and video machines, you had your eyes closed 'sometimes,' and you were being assaulted."

He paused to give the jury a chance to consider and digest the circumstances surrounding the rape.

"Given these conditions," he went on, "can you truly say—*truly say*—how many voices you heard or where they were coming from?"

She glanced helplessly at Katheryn, then said very quietly, "No."

"Well, then, Miss Tobias," Wainwright asked, his voice butterscotch smooth, "is it fair to say that you can't truly tell us who shouted or applauded? Is that fair?"

She glared at him before she gave her answer. "Yes, that's fair."

Wainwright smiled, bowed his head modestly, and exchanged places with his colleague, Dan Paulsen, who was representing Stuart Holloway.

Paulsen walked with a pronounced limp. He hobbled up to the front of the courtroom and began abruptly. "Miss Tobias, while you were on the pinball machine, did you at any time cry 'Help' or 'Rape'?"

"I tried," Sarah said defiantly, "but they were always covering my mouth. They had their hands over my mouth, or they were kissing me, and . . . and I kept saying 'No.' "

Paulsen limped back a few steps. " 'No'?"

"Yes. I mean, yes, I said 'No.' "

"Not 'Rape' or 'Help' or 'Police' . . . but . . . 'No'?"

"Right—'No.' "

"Did anyone hear you?"

"I don't know," she said irritably.

"Did you signal to anybody in the room? A hand signal, say?"

"My hands were pinned down, okay?" she flared.

Paulsen acknowledged his mistake with an apologetic nod. "Did you signal to anybody with your eyes?"

"No."

"Were you struggling?"

"Yes."

"Did anyone see you struggling?"

"They must have," Sarah said sullenly, put off by his dry, rapid-fire manner.

Paulsen stared piercingly at the jury, as if to say,

"Pay close attention. This is the important part." Then he said, "Miss Tobias, can you in any way prove to us that someone in that room, anyone, heard you saying 'No' or saw you struggling?"

Sarah took a long time to answer. She felt as if Paulsen were trying to trick her into admitting something he could use against her. Philip Joyce had told Katheryn that *he* had seen her struggling, but it was up to him to tell that to the court.

She looked to Katheryn for guidance. She seemed to be saying to Sarah, *Tell the truth, but be careful.*

Finally, she gazed back at Paulsen and told him, "No."

Paulsen waited a moment to allow the jury to consider her response. "No more questions," he said finally.

Katheryn was immediately up on her feet for the redirect. "Miss Tobias," she said, "while you were being gang-raped on that pinball machine, what were you thinking?"

"Thinking?"

"Yes, what were you thinking? What words popped into your head?"

She stared at Katheryn, bewildered. "Words?"

"Yes—words. Three men were repeatedly raping you, holding you down, while their friends clapped and cheered—"

"Your Honor!" Paulsen jumped up and exclaimed.

Katheryn ignored his attempt to register an objection. "And you lay there, naked and defenseless, weeping, struggling, every part of you in pain. What words popped into your head?"

Her voice rose to a crescendo as she all but shouted at Sarah, "What words?"

Goaded by Katheryn, Sarah forgot that she was sitting in a courtroom, safe from harm. Suddenly she was back there again, held prisoner on the glass top of the pinball machine, crying out for help.

"No!" she screamed. "No! No! No!"

CHAPTER SIXTEEN

THE NEXT MORNING SARAH SURPRISED BOTH HERself and Katheryn when she showed up at Katheryn's office with two cardboard cups of coffee and a bag of doughnuts.

"I hope you like it black," she said.

"I do. Thanks," said Katheryn, looking up from her work and pantomiming shock.

Sarah sat down. Whether or not Katheryn believed in the power of the planets, Sarah knew they exerted an influence. She had worked out Katheryn's horoscope. Now she said casually, "You know, Leos frighten off friends as well as enemies, so today you have to—"

But Katheryn shook her head wearily. "Not now, please, Sarah."

"Hey, I'm sorry." Sarah fidgeted with her earrings. "But can I ask you one question?"

"One," Katheryn said, smiling.

"Was I okay yesterday?"

Katheryn knew what an effort that had cost Sarah. "Not okay," Katheryn replied, stone-faced. "Not okay—terrific!" she continued, breaking into a wide grin.

Sarah blushed with pleasure. "Hey! You know, you were—"

But Katheryn stopped Sarah with a warning finger to her lips and pointed to the open door. Several moments later there was a knock. Paul Rudolph appeared in the doorway, with Philip Joyce in tow.

Paul nodded politely to Sarah, then turned to Philip. "Go ahead, Mr. Joyce. Please tell Ms. Murphy and Ms. Tobias what you just told me."

When Philip hesitated, Paul said, "Mr. Joyce has just told me that he doesn't truly remember the events of the night in question and that he only told you what he told you because you coerced him. He says if you put him on the stand he will recant. He will take it all back."

"Did you do this?" Katheryn demanded angrily.

Paul ignored her question and said coldly, "I'd suggest you notify the court and the defense that he won't be testifying. In fact," he gloated, turning to leave the office, "it might be less . . . awkward . . . if you moved for immediate dismissal."

Philip was about to follow him, but Katheryn said coldly, "Please wait a moment, Mr. Joyce. If you're not going to testify, I need you to sign an instrument to that effect."

Don't blame him, she told herself. *That son of a*

bitch Rudolph must have somehow gotten to him. She should have figured that he'd have to come up with something to punish her for her show of independence. And Philip was an easy mark, because he was obviously scared and reluctant to testify. The district attorney had provided him with the perfect way out.

Glad for an excuse to leave the room before she lashed out at Philip, she got up to find a blank testimony waiver. Her high heels clicked angrily against the tile floor as she walked out of the office without another word.

Sarah, on the other hand, had no such compunctions. Philip had double-crossed her, and she needed to know why. As soon as they were alone, she turned on him.

"Why?" she challenged him.

Philip frowned unhappily. "I don't remember what happened," he said unconvincingly, "and I only said what I did because that lady lawyer forced me to, and if she makes me take the stand I'll take it all back."

He wasn't going to get off the hook that easily. Sarah had to know why he was doing this to her, so she repeated in the same unyielding voice, "Why?"

"I told you, I don't remember." Philip raised his voice defiantly.

"You're full of shit."

Stung by her contempt, Philip hit back. "Who the hell are *you* to tell me I'm full of shit? I was there, remember?"

"Right, you were there," Sarah snapped. "And you saw me have a few drinks, and you saw me blow some grass, and you saw me flirt and dance—and then you saw me gang-raped, and you think I had it coming. You're just like the others!"

She turned her back to him so that he couldn't see her tears.

"Look," Philip said pleadingly, trying to get her to understand, "my best friend is in prison, and if I do this, they'll keep him for—"

Sarah whirled around. "I get it. I get it. Your best friend is such a great guy, and I'm just this lowlife whore he raped right in front of you. I get it," she spat. "You're *not* like the others. You're worse!"

"I am not! I am not!" Philip shouted, pounding his fist against Katheryn's desk.

Suddenly Sarah understood. She had been there before herself. Leaning forward, she touched his knee and said softly, "Hey, it's okay to be scared."

CHAPTER SEVENTEEN

ONCE PHILIP PROMISED SARAH HE WOULD TESTIFY on her behalf, he felt a tremendous burden lifted from his shoulders. "Sarah Tobias, victim" had been transformed in his mind into Sarah Tobias, someone who, in spite of her own pain, could reach out to comfort him. She hadn't once asked him why he hadn't come forward earlier, and he was grateful to her for that.

He was also grateful, as he walked through the courtroom to the witness box, that Bob would not be present for his testimony. Certainly Bob would find out soon enough about whatever Philip said today in court. But Philip preferred not to have his friend staring at him accusingly from the audience.

The court officer swore him in and then told him, "You may take the stand."

Katheryn looked her typically calm, self-assured self as she walked to the front of the room. Nobody would have ever guessed that she had hardly closed her eyes the night before, so preoccupied with worrying about whether she had covered every angle of the case.

She had explained to Philip that her first few questions were meant to establish the facts for the judge and jury. Now she took a deep breath and said, "Can you tell us your name?"

Philip gulped nervously. "Philip Joyce."

"Were you in the Mill on the night of the events involving Sarah Tobias?" she asked.

"Yes," Philip replied.

Now she said, just as she had told him she would, "Would you please recount what happened?"

Philip gulped again. And then he began to describe his memory of the events of that night. "Well, it was late, and me and my friend Bob, we'd been to a game, and then he took me to this bar he sometimes goes to, the Mill. We'd been there a while, just hanging out, when this girl came in. She was real sexy . . . pretty."

Katheryn nodded to him to continue.

"So she was sitting in a booth talking to her friend when this guy Danny—he was sitting at the end of the bar—he saw her come in, too—and he sent the bartender over with some drinks."

Listening from her seat in the first row, Sarah thought, *Yes, that's how it was.*

She and Sally had been sitting in the booth, having a little fun, checking out the two kids in the booth next to theirs. She had made that crack about taking Bob home, but she was only joking—he had a nice body, and she was mad at Larry. But she never would have really gone through with it. It was only talk.

Then Jesse brought them over a couple of beers—"compliments of the guy at the bar," he said—and then the guy walked over and sat down next to her. He had curly dark hair, a cute smile, a cute ass.

Sally introduced them. "Danny, this is my friend Sarah."

Sarah lifted her glass. "Hey, Danny, thanks."

"You two talkin' shop?"

They started giggling like two schoolkids, and she winked at him and said, "Modern romances."

Danny shrugged. "Hey, I'm a romantic. I'm like you, Sarah. I mean, you are one romantic-looking girl."

She knew he was handing her a line, but that was more than Larry ever said, and it felt pretty good. So she wasn't too thrilled when one of the Mill regulars, Angela, stopped at their booth and said, "Danny, it's your turn."

"A romantic, huh?" Sarah hooted.

Danny looked almost hurt. "She's not with me. She came in with somebody else. Hey," he said when she looked at him skeptically, "don't take my word for it. Walk back and see for yourself."

Philip must have been watching her the whole time, because he described the scene just as it had happened: "Then she got up and followed him into the game room, and pretty soon they were playing pinball with Bob and getting really loaded."

She and Danny were drinking beers and playing pinball when the cute college kid came over and asked if he could play.

Danny stuck another quarter in the slot, and she sent the ball careening through the plastic gates. Lights were flashing, and all the bells were going off—*bing, bing, bing*—one after another, and then the ball slammed into the winning hole.

"Hey, hey, hey," she shouted.

Danny slapped her a high five. "You guys might as well pay up now, 'cause she can score," he bragged.

"Luck," scoffed Kurt, tapping the pinball machine with his pool cue.

"Luck, my ass. You wish," she jeered good-humoredly.

Danny patted her ass approvingly. "Quick reflexes. I think we got a champ."

Another quarter in the machine, and she was moving again, about to bring home another win. The crowd was rooting for her, yelling at Bob that he could never beat her, he might as well pack it in, she was too good . . .

Just as a joke, playing to the audience, Bob spread his hand over the glass top of the pinball machine, blocking Sarah's view.

"Hey, get your hand off there," she protested. "I'm on a roll!"

She sank another ball, and Angela applauded. "Looks like her arm's connected to her ass."

But her lucky streak ended right then, and she missed a shot. Bob let out a triumphant yell. Pretending to pout, Sarah grabbed Danny's glass out of his hand and leaned into him as he slipped his arm around her waist.

"Hey, Angie, put some music on," Bob shouted, taking his turn at the machine.

Sarah fished a joint out of her purse, lit it up, and inhaled deeply.

"Keep that all to yourself?" Danny coaxed.

"You want my paycheck, too?"

He smirked. "If you want to give it to me."

"You're funny." She moved away from him and began to dance by herself. "Oh, man, I love this song."

Danny walked over and began dancing with her. A few of the customers drifted back to the bar to watch the wrestling match on TV, but the rest stayed in the game room, shooting pool and playing video games.

Kurt poked Bob in the arm. "Hey, Bobby, what's happenin'?"

"She is, man. Check it out." He gestured toward Sarah and Danny who were folded in each other's arms.

"I've got to work lunch tomorrow," Sarah was saying, but Danny wasn't listening. He nuzzled her neck and kissed her. "Ooh, watch your mouth," she mumbled. "This isn't fair, I'm too gonzo . . . call me at work . . . man, you are one slick cucumber . . ."

"Why waste it?" Danny whispered into her ear. "You don't wanna go home."

Sarah groaned. "No, but I gotta."

"Tomorrow, huh?" He licked her ear persuasively. "Okay. Can we kiss a little?"

She tried to pull away, protesting weakly, "You are so bogus."

"I swear," he murmured. "Just a little."

He pulled her head back by her hair and kissed her again, then slid his hand beneath her sweatshirt. Sarah tried to resist, but she was too stoned to put up much of a fight.

"Tomorrow," she mumbled, batting at him. "Tomorrow."

Danny pulled her closer to him, all the while whispering that he wanted to kiss her, to touch her, just a little. She would like it, he promised her, just a little . . .

She shook her head no, no . . .

Yes, Danny nodded, yes . . . just a little kiss . . .

"They were kissing," Philip told the court, "but then she tried to pull away. But he was too strong, and he pushed her down on the pinball machine and ripped down her top and pushed up her skirt."

Her head and back were pressed against the hard glass top of the machine. Danny had pulled her skirt all the way off and pushed her underpants down to her knees. With one hand on her neck, he held her head down as he kissed her.

"Hey, my man!" Cliff whooped, catching a glimpse. "Going after new blood! You're our man, Danny!"

Drawn by Cliff's cries, the other men moved closer to get a better view.

Sally was standing in the doorway of the game room, talking to one of the customers, when she caught a glimpse of Sarah, flat on her back, with Danny bent over her.

She turned away in disgust and went over to the bar to retrieve her coat.

"Where are you going?" Jesse asked her.

"Home! I don't like the show in there," she said, angry at Sarah for getting so stoned and drunk that she didn't realize she was making a fool of herself just to get back at Larry.

Jesse shrugged and went back to watching the boxing match. But Arthur Polito, his curiosity piqued, sauntered over to see what all the excitement was about. He elbowed his way through the crowd, just as Bob stepped forward and ripped off Sarah's underpants.

Cliff, Matt, and Stu were egging Danny on with cries of "Oh yeah! All right! C'mon, man, give it to her!" Their screams of excitement all but drowned out the music from the other room.

As Danny shuddered to a climax, Cliff shouted at Bob, "Hey, college boy, it's your turn!"

"Yeah," Danny chimed in, proudly acknowledging the cheers of the other men. "It's your shot, Bobby. Can you handle it?"

Matt shoved Bob forward, growling, "Go get her, frat boy!"

By now Philip had edged closer, in time to catch a glimpse of his friend grabbing Sarah's thighs and mounting her. Earlier, Philip and Bob had noticed Sarah and her girlfriend, giggling and staring at Bob. So now Bob was going to get a little action.

He had said he wanted to get laid tonight . . .

Still, Philip thought there was something pathetic about the sight of Sarah, flat on her back, her legs dangling helplessly over the side of the machine. And with all the guys standing around and watching, it didn't seem right . . .

From behind the bar Jesse could hear the fevered cries of excitement. His view was blocked by the crowd gathered in the doorway, but he hoped nothing too weird was going on in there. The cops sometimes stopped by for a quick shot or a cup of coffee, and the liquor commissioner wasn't real big on bars featuring live sex acts.

One of the men came over to order another whiskey.

"What's goin' on?" Jesse asked, pouring his drink.

The customer winked and moved his fist back and forth.

Jesse got the picture right away. "Oh, for Chrissake," he swore. If the boys didn't cut it out real soon, he'd have to go on in there and break it up himself. Not that he gave a good goddamn what they did to get their rocks off, but it would be on his head if things got out of control. Shit! What he didn't have to do to earn a living!

Bob was making the most of his time with Sarah. She squirmed wildly, fighting to get out from under him, but no way was he going to let her go before he was done. His reputation with the townies was riding on this. He gripped her legs tightly and moved himself back and forth inside her, in time to the music.

"Hey, hey, hey," Matt crowed. "Bet you can't do it to the music, Bobby!"

Bob kept thrusting, all the while trying to kiss her, but she tossed her head from side to side to avoid his mouth.

"No!" she cried over and over again. "No! No!"

But Sarah's protests went unheard, drowned out by the din of the music and the boisterous shouts of the audience. She flailed her arms violently and clawed at the faces of the men positioned around her, struggling to get free.

"Hold her down, hold her down!" Stu yelled.

Shocked by Stu's belligerent cry, Philip spun around and took a closer look. The girl wasn't doing this willingly, he realized with a sickening jolt. What was happening here was nothing short of rape. He leaned closer and saw that she was trying to protest, "No! No! No!"

But either he was the only one in the room who knew what was going on, or nobody else gave a damn that a violent, ugly assault was taking place here.

"She's ready to come!" Cliff shouted.

"Stick it to her!" screamed Matt. "Don't slip out!"

"Not my buddy," Danny roared. "Go, Bobby! Shit, he's turning me on! Hey, you too, Kurt?"

By now, more of the onlookers had caught on to what Philip had already figured out—that Sarah was not a willing participant in this entertainment. They glanced uneasily at one another, and a few of them shamefacedly slunk back to the bar.

Cliff slapped his thigh, his face red with excitement. "Make her moan! Oh yeah! Watch the kid, Kurt," he teased. "You might learn something!"

"Shut the fuck up, asshole!" snarled Kurt.

"Listen to needle dick!" Cliff taunted him.

Matt had to throw in his two cents. "You gonna let him talk to you like that?"

His masculinity challenged, Kurt had no choice but to step forward, grinning lustily, to take his turn.

"C'mon," Danny urged Bob. "Kurt's waiting in line."

Kurt pulled Bob away. He staggered backward, and loud applause filled the room. A satisfied smile plastered across his face, he collapsed theatrically against one of the pinball machines.

Stu, Cliff, and Matt began to chant in rhythmic unison, "Kurt, Kurt, Kurt, Kurt, Kurt!"

"Here comes the champ!" Stu announced as Danny grabbed hold of Sarah's hands and Kurt unzipped his fly.

"He fucks like a moose," guffawed Cliff.

"Keep it comin', keep it comin'," Matt goaded Kurt, though by now Kurt needed no urging.

It could have been a football game, and the three of them the cheerleading squad, rooting their team on to the finish line—to victory. Cliff shouting and clapping in time to the music. Matt yelling, "Do it, do it, do it!" Stu screaming, "Harder, harder, harder!"

"She was being raped," Philip said in voice choked with emotion, speaking so quietly that the courtroom spectators had to strain to hear him. "And all these people were watching, and these guys were cheering and laughing."

Cliff led the chorus, with Matt and Stu joining in loudly. "One, two, three, four, fuck that pussy 'til it's sore! One, two, three, four, fuck that pussy 'til it's sore! One, two, three, four, fuck that pussy 'til it's sore!"

Their insane chant propelled Philip into action. He shoved his way through the men and bolted toward the front door, just as the music on the jukebox came to an abrupt halt.

The men's frenzied shouts and applause rang out clearly, underscored by Sarah's strangled, piteous wail: "No . . . no . . . no . . . no . . ."

Puzzled by the noise, Jesse lowered the volume on the TV.

Sarah's cries became more audible. "No . . . no . . . no . . . no . . . !"

"Knock it off! You hear me, knock it off!" Jesse shouted furiously. "Go home if you wanna fuck!"

His angry words struck the men like a blast of cold water. Kurt loosened his hold on Sarah. She immediately clamped her teeth down on his hand and kicked him so hard he lost his balance. Quickly she managed to get to her feet and stumbled out of the room, wearing only her pink sweatshirt.

The place fell silent as Sarah staggered past the bar and through the door.

"No!" she screamed. "No!"

CHAPTER EIGHTEEN

THE RAINSTORM THAT HAD BEEN THREATENING through the morning finally hit with all the fury that the black clouds and wind had promised. Except for Philip's sobs, the only noise that could be heard in the hushed courtroom was the sound of raindrops pounding against the windows.

There was a roll of thunder, then several seconds later an accompanying flash of lightning. One of the jury members jumped in fright, but otherwise nobody moved.

Katheryn waited patiently for Philip to regain his composure. Even she, who had already heard his story, had found the recitation harrowing. She could imagine the pain he must be feeling now as she asked him to recall the events in every excruciating detail.

But his pain could never compare to the agony of Sarah's ordeal. Katheryn only hoped that the jury had that same realization. She wondered whether the five women jurors were putting themselves in Sarah's place . . . or were they mistakenly thinking, as she had, that they were safe from rape and harassment?

Don't ever believe it, she wanted to tell them. Men like the ones who were being tried in this courtroom didn't wait to be asked. They saw a sexy smile and took that for an open invitation.

That was precisely the point that Katheryn was hoping to impress on the jury. That no woman was any safer than Sarah Tobias until Albrecht and Holloway and Haines, and all the others like them, understood that there was only one universal code of decency.

Philip stared at the rain on the windows and remembered the rain hitting the glass of the phone booth that night. He nodded at Katheryn to signal that he was ready to continue.

"Mr. Joyce," she asked gently, "you called the police?"

"Yeah," he said. "From a phone booth outside the Mill."

"Did you tell the police your name?"

He shook his head no. "Bob is my friend," he said, the excuse sounding weak and hollow in his ears.

"Is that the only reason you didn't give your name?"

"I was scared," he admitted softly.

The court recorder called out, "I didn't hear that."

"I was scared," Philip repeated more loudly, feeling terribly ashamed of himself.

"So you saw three men—Danny, Kurt, and your

friend Bob—rape Miss Tobias on a pinball machine?" Katheryn went on.

"Yes," he replied.

"And you heard other men yelling remarks of encouragement?"

"Yes."

"Can you tell us, please, if any of the men who shouted those remarks are here?"

"Yes."

"Can you point them out, please?"

Katheryn had told him that he would be asked to identify the defendants in court. But the knowledge hadn't prepared him for how difficult this moment would be. To turn and point an accusing finger at the men seated just a short distance away from him . . .

"Those three—there," he said uncomfortably.

His statement was greeted by a noisy rumbling from the audience. The three men sat impassively, but their families whispered urgently, and the spectators in the back rows craned their heads to get a better look.

The judge glared down from the bench, waiting for silence. When the room was quiet again, Katheryn said, "Mr. Joyce, did anyone else in the room shout any remarks?"

"Just Danny."

"Did you?"

"No!" he said emphatically.

"Mr. Joyce, what did Mr. Holloway shout?"

Philip twisted unhappily in his seat, wishing he didn't have to repeat the words he had heard that night at the Mill. The men had made it seem as if

Sarah were nothing more than a slab of meat, to be handled and poked and used any way that suited them.

He cleared his throat nervously. "'Hold her down, hold her down! Go for it!'"

There were shocked murmurs from the audience, but Katheryn ignored them and went on. "And Mr. Haines?"

"'Stick it to her, stick it to her! Don't stop! Don't stop!'"

"And Mr. Albrecht?"

Philip glanced at Sarah, just a few feet away from him. She was crying silently, her tears flowing down her face like a swollen stream overflowing its banks. She had sat in this very same chair and bravely described what they had done to her. What courage that must have taken—more guts than he had shown the night she had been raped.

He forced himself to look directly at Cliff Albrecht and repeated what Albrecht had said: "'Let the frat boy in! Make her moan!' Then everybody was shouting at once, 'Do it, do it, don't stop, don't stop, stick it to her,' and then they started clapping and chanting." He paused and gathered a deep breath before he continued. "'One, two, three, four, poke that pussy 'til it's sore!'"

Philip blinked his eyes rapidly, determined not to cry again. But some of the spectators were sobbing openly. Others laughed nervously, titillated in spite of themselves by the obscenities unexpectedly spoken aloud in the courtroom.

Wainwright and Paulsen sat stone-faced, hardly

blinking an eye. But Jane Meyerhoff, Matthew Haines's attorney, fiddled with her wedding ring, fretfully pushing the band up and down her finger and rubbing her knuckle thoughtfully.

Katheryn stole a sideways look at the jury. Though they were struggling to mask their distress, they were obviously disturbed by Philip's testimony.

She had one more question to put to him. "Mr. Joyce, do you think Sarah Tobias instigated the rape?"

"No," he declared unhesitatingly, glad for the opportunity to put his opinion on record. "No, I don't."

"Thank you, Mr. Joyce," said Katheryn, and she returned to her seat.

By prior agreement, Jane Meyerhoff stood up to cross-examine Philip.

Jane Meyerhoff was a small, prim-looking woman, so plain and colorless that she reminded Katheryn of the sparrows that fluttered about the park. But for all her drab coloration, Jane, like the sparrows, was capable of making a great deal of bothersome noise.

She began her cross-examination calmly, as if the testimony she had just heard had in no way incriminated her client. "Mr. Joyce, apart from Miss Tobias, about how many people were in the pinball machine area?"

Philip shrugged. "Eight, ten maybe."

She stared at him thoughtfully, then turned to face the jury. "You were drinking, and the TV *and* the jukebox were both on?"

"Yes," Philip said uneasily.

"And you're certain you heard Mr. Haines shout, 'Hold her down'?"

Certain . . . "Yes," said Philip after a moment's pause.

Meyerhoff moved another step closer to the jurors and shrugged expressively in their direction. Then she traded places with Wainwright, who vigorously picked up the questioning where she had left off.

"Mr. Joyce," he asked loudly, "while you were both in the game room, did you keep an eye on Bob?"

"Sometimes . . . sure." Philip looked at him, puzzled.

"Mr. Joyce," pressed Wainwright, "have you ever gone to a pornographic movie?"

"Yes," Philip said, embarrassed to have to admit to that.

"Did you watch the screen?"

"Sure," he stammered, thrown off guard by Wainwright's line of questioning.

"Did you watch what other people in the theater were doing?"

"No."

"But at the Mill you only watched your friend Bob 'sometimes'?"

Philip hesitated. "Yes."

Wainwright's delivery was so affable that Philip hardly felt the damage he was inflicting. "Did you at any time watch the other two men at the pinball machine?"

"Yes."

Wainwright rocked back on his heels, moving in for the kill. "Well, where would you say most of your attention was directed—to the pinball machine or to the others in the room?"

"Uh, I'm . . . I'm not sure." Philip faltered.

"But sure enough for you to have told the jury—under oath—what my client supposedly shouted?" asked Wainwright. He stared at Philip, his face a study in incredulity.

Philip stared back. "Yes," he said stubbornly.

"So, at that moment, your attention was not on the pinball machine?"

"That's right."

Wainwright moved closer to the witness box and asked, in a tone that invited confidence and trust, "Not on the pinball machine—where three men, including your friend Bob, were engaged in public sex?"

"I couldn't watch."

"Because it was live rather than a movie?"

"Because it was too ugly," Philip said, with loud emphasis on the last word.

"Ah." Wainwright stroked his chin. "You were . . . offended?"

"They were *raping* her."

"Oh? You paid enough attention to the machine to notice that?"

"Yes."

"And you instantly yelled 'Rape' or 'Stop'?"

"No, I told you that," Philip said miserably.

"That's right." Wainwright nodded agreeably, as if he had forgotten for the moment. "You did. Is it possible someone else could have yelled 'Rape' or 'Stop'?"

"I didn't hear anyone . . ."

"I see," said Wainwright, his tone implying that in

fact he wasn't sure he did see. He shook his head with apparent confusion and took his time returning to the defense table.

Katheryn jiggled her knee anxiously. Wainwright was a clever son of a bitch. She had to hand it to him. He had set up a nasty little trap, and she wasn't altogether sure that Philip wasn't about to get caught in it.

Al had warned her that Paul Rudolph would be in court today. And she knew damn well he wasn't there to offer her moral support. No doubt he would get a perverse pleasure out of seeing his erstwhile protégée fall flat on her face. She had done her best. The rest was up to Philip.

It fell to Dan Paulsen to spring the trap. He limped to the front of the courtroom and nodded at Philip. "Mr. Joyce," he asked in his dry monotone, "on the night of the events in question, did you go back to your fraternity?"

"Yes," Philip replied, looking as guilty as if he were the accused.

Paulsen considered the tips of his long fingers. "Did you sleep?"

"No." He had tossed restlessly all night, haunted by his memories of Sarah's cries.

"Have you had any trouble sleeping since?"

"Yes," he admitted, wondering how Paulsen could have known.

"Have you thought about that night?"

"Sure." For weeks that was all he had thought about. He had tormented himself with the image of Sarah sprawled across the pinball machine. And he had reproached himself ceaselessly for not having come to her rescue.

Paulsen studied him, the scientist studying a specimen that he was having trouble classifying. "Do you still think about it?"

"Yes," Philip said, squirming under his sharp-eyed gaze.

"Would you say you relive the night in your mind?"

"Yes, yes, I do."

"How often?"

Philip paused. ". . . A lot."

"Do you believe all the men in the game room behaved badly?"

"Yes."

"Including you?"

"Yes," he admitted reluctantly. He glanced over at Sarah, but he couldn't read her expression. When they had talked that day in Katheryn's office, he had wanted to say he was sorry. But he couldn't find the words, and then Katheryn had walked back in, and the moment was gone. He hoped she was paying attention now and hearing his confession as a sort of apology.

There was only the faintest hint of disdain in Paulsen's manner when he asked, "You knew she was being raped, and you let it happen?"

"Yes," said Philip, his voice breaking. "God, yes."

"You feel awful about that, don't you?" Paulsen asked kindly.

Philip couldn't restrain his tears as he answered, "Yes, I do."

"Awful enough to testify against these men on behalf of Sarah Tobias?"

"Yes."

"Yet isn't it possible, Mr. Joyce," demanded Paulsen, raising his voice so that not even the people seated in the last rows of the courtroom could miss his point, "that you were the only person in the room to notice that this rape was taking place?"

Suddenly realizing that he had walked right into Paulsen's well-disguised trap, Philip sputtered angrily, "Hell no." He glanced apologetically at the judge. "I'm sorry. No."

"But didn't you tell Ms. Murphy in your first conversation, 'They probably didn't even know what was going down . . . it was like a show'?"

Philip glanced at Katheryn, appealing for help.

But the expression on her face was impenetrable. She couldn't help him now, and she knew it. This was sink-or-swim time. Paulsen had Philip by the throat, but the damage wasn't fatal. All he had to do was tell the truth.

"Didn't you say that, Mr. Joyce?" Paulsen reiterated.

"Yes," Philip acknowledged.

Paulsen sent his arrow zinging home. "Yet you still insist, Mr. Joyce, that these men knew they were watching a rape?"

Philip glanced again at Katheryn, desperate for some small clue to help him avoid Paulsen's treacherous trap. But she gave him back nothing. And then he understood that he had to depend on himself to figure out where he wanted to go and how to get there.

That was the message Katheryn was sending him. That he had to trust himself. The realization was exhilarating. He looked at the jurors, who were hanging on his response, and then at the defendants.

"Yes," he said. "They knew."

"No further questions," Paulsen said with a cynical, disbelieving smile.

Katheryn had been biding her time impatiently, waiting for the redirect. As soon as Paulsen turned away, she jumped to her feet.

"Mr. Joyce," she asked, "have you told the jury the truth about what you saw and what you heard in that pinball room?"

"Yes," Philip replied without a tremor of doubt.

"Thank you." She nodded to the judge that she was finished with the witness.

The judge told Philip he could step down and signaled the officer to escort him out of the courtroom. His legs stiff with the suppressed tension of the last hour, Philip kept his eyes averted as he walked past the defendants' table and down the aisle. But he couldn't resist taking a quick look at Sarah. The look on her face told him he had made it to the finish line.

The judge looked expectantly at Katheryn.

"The people rest," she told him. She took her seat and waited to see what surprises the defense team had in store for her.

She was prepared for their first witness. Sarah had heard through the grapevine that they would be calling Larry to testify against her. But Katheryn could impugn his credibility by mentioning his drug busts and his failed relationship with Sarah.

Just as she had expected, Paulsen stood up and announced, "The defense calls Lawrence Rydell."

A moment later Larry was escorted into the courtroom. Sarah stared at him in amazement as he was sworn in. Her ex-boyfriend had been transformed from a greasy-haired, stoned biker masquerading as a musician into the sort of neatly dressed young man a mother would be pleased to have her daughter bring home.

She wondered what he could possibly have to say that could be used against her. She didn't have to wait long to find out.

Paulsen got straight to the point. He asked, "When Miss Tobias came home the night of April eighteenth and she told you this horrible story, you didn't completely believe her?"

Larry carefully avoided looking in Sarah's direction as he answered Paulsen's question. He waved his hand dismissively and said, "Nah, she kinda lives a lot in her own head, ya know what I'm sayin'?"

Paulsen nodded smugly and took his seat without another word.

It took Katheryn a moment or two to realize that Paulsen had nothing further to ask his witness. *Good,* she thought. The real work would come later on, when they called Sally. Larry Rydell was a piece of cake.

She approached the witness box and fixed him with what Al Massi called her "strict-as-a-schoolmarm look."

"Mr. Rydell," she said, "on the night of April eighteenth, when Miss Tobias said she was going to the Mill for a drink, did you believe her?"

Larry shrugged. "Sure, but—"

"And when she told you why she was going out, did you believe her?"

Larry hesitated, and Katheryn said smoothly, "Let me rephrase it, Mr. Rydell. When she told you she was going out because she couldn't take any more of your lies about your cheating on her, did you believe her?"

Suddenly Larry lost his air of bravado. He looked over at Paulsen, signaling for help. But Paulsen, earlier so solicitous, suddenly had nothing to offer him in the face of Katheryn's imaginative cross-examination.

"Did you believe her?" Katheryn pressed him.

"I guess."

"And the day she asked you to leave her home, did you believe her?"

"Yeah," he said sullenly. "I believed her."

"Mr. Rydell, apart from the night of April eighteenth, can you give us one other example of when you didn't believe Miss Tobias?"

"Sure . . ." He gnawed at his fingernails, already bitten to the quick, as he racked his brain to recall another example. This was what he got, he thought, for letting the lawyers talk him into getting back at Sarah by testifying against her.

"We're waiting, Mr. Rydell," Katheryn crisply reminded him.

He glared at her with poorly disguised resentment. "I can't think of anything right this minute."

"Even though you say Miss Tobias 'kinda lives a lot in her own head,' the only time you didn't believe her was the night she told you she was raped?"

"I can't think of anything this minute," he said again.

So much for Larry Rydell, Katheryn thought gleefully. "No further questions," she told the Judge.

Katheryn hurried out of the courtroom without bothering to look for Al or Dunc. If they had bad news about the day's session, she didn't want to hear it. But Sarah had moved almost as quickly and intercepted her in the parking lot.

Sarah had her own ideas about who had come out ahead today, but she wanted an expert's opinion. "So?" she asked, not bothering with any formalities.

Katheryn decided to give it to her straight. "Philip helped. Larry? Sort of—maybe. Jesse—also sort of."

"What about Sally? Bad, huh?"

"Bad."

Sarah kicked at the gravel with the toe of her shoe. "Shit," she swore.

"Shit," Katheryn agreed.

"You wanna go for a drink?" Sarah suggested.

"I have to put together a summation," said Katheryn, thinking how badly she could use a drink to smooth out the edges, as Sarah liked to put it.

She smiled regretfully as she unlocked the car door and got inside. But Sarah wasn't ready to let her go just yet. There was more she needed to know from Katheryn. She didn't even have to put the question into words. The look in her eye was enough.

"Fifty-fifty," Katheryn said as gently as she could. "At best."

It was about what Sarah expected, but she had hoped that Katheryn might be more optimistic. She masked her disappointment with a quick nod and began to walk away. Suddenly, remembering what else she wanted to say to Katheryn, she turned back.

"Wear something gold tomorrow," she instructed her. "It's Leo's color."

"Sarah," Katheryn said, exasperated, "that's not—"

"Trust me for once," Sarah told her firmly. "Gold."

Katheryn didn't hear the alarm go off the next morning, which in itself was unusual. On days when she was due in court she normally was awake and out of bed long before her clock radio clicked itself on. But this morning, of all mornings, she slept through it, until somewhere deep in her REM state, the disc jockey announced that it was almost eight-thirty.

She had barely enough time to shower and get dressed and get to court by nine-thirty. And without her mandatory cup of black coffee she felt as if she were moving in slow motion. She knew that as soon as she had to face the jury with her summation the adrenaline would begin to flow, and she would be fine. But in the meantime it was all she could do to get out of her apartment in one piece.

She checked herself in the full-length mirror before she dashed out the door. Her shoes were polished, no runs in her pantyhose, no stains on her shirt, and her suit was clean and pressed. On a last-minute impulse, she pinned her grandmother's amber-and-gold brooch on her lapel.

The atmosphere in the courtroom was even more highly charged than it had been on the previous days of the trial. Sensing that today's oral summations would be a dramatic, high-stakes battle, the media had turned out in full force. Every seat was spoken for, and several disappointed would-be spectators had to be turned away because there weren't enough seats in the courtroom.

As the judge entered the courtroom on the dot of nine-thirty, the officer went through the opening rituals that signaled the beginning of yet another day in court. Then the judge looked over at the defense table and said, "Gentlemen . . ."

Dan Paulsen stood up and approached the bench.

"Your Honor," Paulsen said, "my colleagues have agreed to a single summation."

The judge glanced questioningly at Katheryn, who said, "No objection."

Paulsen slowly made his way over to the jury box and nodded gravely at the jurors.

"Ladies and gentlemen," he began, "the state has charged these three men with a crime, and the state has supported its charge with the testimony of two witnesses. Sarah Tobias told you how three men raped her. Then she told you that she heard other men shouting encouragement to her attackers. Did she name these other men? No. Did she describe these other men? No. Could she tell you what these other men shouted? No. Her sworn testimony, her poignant, heartrending sworn testimony, was an appeal to your pity. And if her story is true, you should pity her. But even if her story is true, and you do pity her, it has nothing to do with this case . . . because *those* three men"—he pointed at the defendants—"did not rape her.

"Her sworn testimony is nothing, and you must treat it as nothing. If you wish," Paulsen laughed grimly, "you can also treat as nothing the testimony of her lover, Larry, who described to you what kind of woman she is; and you can treat as nothing the testimony of the bartender, Jesse, who told you she was so drunk she could barely stand; and you can even treat as nothing the testimony of her friend, Sally, who told you of Miss Tobias's intentions that night. Our case does not depend on those witnesses, just as the people's case does not depend on Sarah Tobias."

Sarah could hear her heart pounding in the stillness of the room. Paulsen droned on, but she hardly heard his words. His voice was just so much background noise, like the sound of the TV at the Dugout—annoying but unimportant.

Of much greater importance were the impassive faces staring out from the jury box. How strange it felt, after all these months of waiting, to have the fate of her case come down to the unanimous decision of these twelve men and women.

Paulsen paused and regarded the jurors. "The people's case depends on Philip Joyce. If you believe him, you will convict those three men. If you do not, you will acquit them.

"*Do* you believe him? Why did Philip Joyce testify?

Why did a man who cold-bloodedly watched a rape, who hid like a rat in a cellar for months, who could not drag himself to court until he was confronted with Sarah Tobias . . . why did this man testify?

"Ladies and gentlemen," Paulsen declared dramatically, confident that he had captured them with his rhetoric, "there is guilt in this courtroom, and we all know where it lies . . . inside the head of Philip Joyce. Every day for months he said to himself, 'I am guilty,' and finally he was offered a way to purge his guilt, and he took it. He told you he watched a rape . . . and he told you that others in that room watched a rape. But how did he know that? Did he read their minds? To solicit a crime, you must *know* that it *is* a crime. Who knew it? Philip Joyce. Do you think it matters to Philip Joyce who shouted? In his head, everyone in that room is guilty . . . he *told* you that. And Philip Joyce, who *is* guilty, who *did* watch a rape and do nothing, will purge himself by bringing down anyone who was in that room with him."

Paulsen laughed harshly. "At no legal cost to himself . . . while those three men face prison."

He limped back to the defense table and took a sip of water.

"Do you believe him?" he continued after a long, hard look at the jurors. "If you do, convict. If you don't—and I know you don't—acquit."

He bowed brusquely, then walked slowly back to join his colleagues.

Not bad, Katheryn thought as Paulsen took his seat. But not great. She had her own prepared summation, of course, but Paulsen had opened up a few interesting paths for her to explore with the jury. And if she were persuasive enough, those paths would lead them to the verdict she sought.

In her rush earlier to get to her seat before the judge arrived, she hadn't noticed whether Paul was here today. She hoped he was, so that he could hear what would probably be her final oral summation for the D.A.'s office.

Katheryn's voice betrayed neither anxiety nor doubt. She spoke in a quiet, conversational tone, as if the jurors were friends who would understand what she was about to tell them.

"Ladies, gentlemen," she reminded them, "Mr. Paulsen has told you that the testimony of Sarah Tobias is nothing. Sarah Tobias was raped, but that is nothing. She was bruised and cut and terrorized. That is nothing. All of it happened in front of a howling crowd, and that is nothing."

She smiled softly, trusting them enough to confide in them. "Well, it may be nothing to Mr. Paulsen, but it is *not* nothing to Sarah Tobias. And I don't believe it is nothing to you.

"Next," she continued, "Mr. Paulsen tried to convince you that Philip Joyce was the only person in that bar who knew that Sarah Tobias was being raped. The only one.

"You watched Philip Joyce," Katheryn said, moving a step closer to the jury box. "How did he strike you? Did he seem especially sensitive? Especially observant? Did he seem so remarkable that you immediately said to yourselves, 'Of course. This man would notice things other people would not'?"

Pointing at Philip, she asked, "Do you believe that Philip Joyce saw something those three men didn't see? That Philip Joyce and Philip Joyce alone saw the expression on Sarah Tobias's face, saw the thrashing of her legs, saw her nails gash her own hand and draw her own blood? In all the time Sarah Tobias was held down on a pinball machine, they didn't know?"

Of course not, her bleak smile told them. "Because," she continued, "wouldn't it be easy for us if they hadn't known? Then we could pretend that a bunch of drunken men simply watched a bit of group sex, and it would be easy to nod and say, 'People don't do that, they don't stand around while a sickening crime is taking place. They step in. They cry "Stop!" They call for help.'"

She paused long enough to give them a chance to consider her suggestion. "Don't they?" she repeated.

Several of the jurors as well as a few of the spectators nodded their agreement. Katheryn turned and slowly swept the room with her eyes, then turned back to the jurors.

"Is there nobody in this courtroom," she asked them, as if she truly expected an answer, "who has ever watched a crime and done nothing? There's certainly no law against standing around, watching some troubled soul on the ledge of a twenty-story building. But what if the observers yell, 'Jump, jump!' until the troubled soul jumps and dives. Is that a crime?"

She could feel them listening to her, following her, agreeing with her. Their attention excited her, as it always did, and gave her the power to convince them that what she was saying was right and just.

"If someone asked the onlookers if yelling 'Jump, jump!' caused the leap, one guesses they would say, 'Of course not. The guy was crazy. Yelling had *nothing* to do with it.'

"*Nothing* to do with it . . . we're back to nothing. Philip Joyce confessed to you that he watched a rape and did nothing. He told you that everyone in that room behaved badly, and he is right. But—no matter how immoral it may be—it is not the crime of criminal solicitation to walk away from a rape. It is not the crime of criminal solicitation to silently watch a rape. But it *is* the crime of criminal solicitation to entreat, or induce, or encourage, or persuade another person to commit a rape."

She whirled around suddenly and began to shout, "Make her moan! Hold her down! Stick it to her!"

Then she lowered her voice and went on, "Those three men did worse than nothing. They cheered, and they clapped, and they rooted the others on. They made sure Sarah Tobias was raped. And raped. And raped. Now." She paused. "You tell me, is that *nothing?*"

No matter how many trials she had argued—and won—Katheryn invariably felt nervous and despondent as she waited for the jury to come back with their verdict. And the longer they took, the more she fretted and sulked.

To pass the time, she worked on puzzles, the more challenging the better.

But this afternoon the puzzles weren't working their sedativelike magic. Four hours had passed since she had concluded her summation, and the judge had charged the members of the jury with the responsibility of returning a verdict. Four hours that felt like four days.

Ignoring Katheryn's warning that she wasn't fit company, Sarah had insisted on joining her in the empty courtroom she had staked out to do her waiting. The room was cloudy with Sarah's cigarette smoke. She had gone through a pack since lunch.

Spread out in front of her on the table was an overflowing ashtray, her astrology books, and the chart she had begun for one of her friends. But she, too, was having trouble concentrating. The hours seemed to be dragging by, without any sign of whether or not the jury had believed her and Philip Joyce.

"What time is it?" she asked Katheryn.

Katheryn didn't bother to look up. "You just asked me what—"

She was interrupted by a court officer who stuck his head in the door and said, "They want Joyce's testimony read to them again."

"That's the third time for him," Sarah said, lighting another cigarette. "How come they never asked for mine?"

"Because they believed yours," Katheryn replied tersely. She went back to her puzzle, and Sarah to her chart. But five minutes later, forgetting that she had just asked, Sarah sighed anxiously and said, "What time is it?"

"They've been out three hours and twelve minutes," Katheryn said, trying hard not to lose her temper. She understood how interminable the wait felt, but this must be the fourth time in an hour that Sarah had asked her the same question.

What Sarah really wanted to do was present Katheryn with the natal chart she had constructed for her. She had started it weeks ago but hadn't finished it until late last night. She had never worked so hard on any other chart, and it seemed a fitting gift to thank Katheryn for all her help.

But Sarah couldn't think how to present her with the chart. In her head she rehearsed two or three short speeches, then gave up and blurted out, "I did your chart."

She found the piece of paper in her bag and put it down in front of Katheryn. "It's a great chart," she said. "Saturn in the tenth house—career and ambition; Mercury ruling the tenth—public work; Sun and Pluto in the tenth—law and higher understanding. I mean, the tenth house is really gangbusters. You can be president or something."

Something in her tone caught Katheryn's attention as she realized for the first time that Sarah believed—*really* believed—in all this. And just now, she had sounded so sure of herself, as if she knew what she was talking about.

"What about you? What's your future?" asked Katheryn, curious in spite of herself.

"I don't have mine with me," Sarah said fliply.

"Don't you remember it?"

"It's mostly seventh house—intuition, feelings, faith, mystery . . . real useful shit," said Sarah self-mockingly.

Katheryn picked up her chart and examined it. The markings looked incomprehensible, but also pretty, in a mysterious sort of way. "Do I have any of that?"

"A bit," Sarah pointed. "Right here." She paused. "It's for you," she continued. "I didn't sign it 'cause . . . well, you know, you think—"

"Sarah," Katheryn said, grabbing her pen, "will you please sign this damn thing?"

How strange, she thought, watching Sarah sign the bottom of the chart, the way she and Sarah had come together. Thrown together because of a terrible, ugly crime, they had become—not friends, exactly—but two women who had developed a respect for and understanding of each other.

Katheryn had learned a lesson or two from Sarah. She hoped Sarah felt the same about her.

"Thank you." Katheryn smiled, admiring the chart.

"Likewise," Sarah said shyly.

The officer stuck his head in the doorway. "They're coming in," he said.

They took with them into the courtroom the moment they had just shared, a brief but powerful connection—their talisman.

CHAPTER NINETEEN

THE JURORS FILED IN, ONE BY ONE. KATHERYN studied their faces, but they gave away no clues to the verdict they had arrived at. Her nerves were strung so tautly that she started when someone tapped her on the shoulder. It was Dunc, seated just behind her. He winked, and she smiled, grateful for his show of support.

The court officer asked them all to rise as the judge hurried in and took his seat.

He put on his glasses and looked over at the jury box. "Ladies and gentlemen, have you reached a verdict?"

The foreman stood up and announced, "We have, Your Honor."

The judge quickly perused the three slips of paper on which the verdicts had been noted.

Then he said, "Will the defendants please rise and face the jury?"

The three men got to their feet, looking pale and serious. Even Cliff Albrecht, for once, seemed uncharacteristically subdued.

The judge nodded at the foreman to proceed.

The foreman cleared his throat. He said, "We find the defendant Matthew Haines guilty of criminal solicitation."

Haines's mother moaned and began to cry loudly, while his father and other family members muttered their displeasure with the verdict.

The judge banged his gavel and sternly called for order in the court.

The foreman continued, "We find the defendant Clifford Albrecht guilty of criminal solicitation."

Barbara Albrecht cried out, "Oh no!" and once again the judge ordered silence in the courtroom.

He signaled to the foreman to read the third verdict.

The foreman cleared his throat again. "We find the defendant Stuart Holloway guilty of criminal solicitation."

Now not even the pounding of the judge's gavel could contain the angry, pained reactions of the three families. As armed officers moved toward the defendants, their loved ones loudly broadcast their dissatisfaction with the verdicts.

Glancing around, Katheryn unexpectedly found herself the focus of their fury and hatred. She quickly turned face forward toward the bench, where the judge was demanding that there be silence in his courtroom.

"Sentences will be imposed two weeks from today,

at ten," he announced brusquely. He banged his gavel one last time.

Court was adjourned.

Katheryn stood up to go and found herself looking at Paul Rudolph. To her astonishment and chagrin, he gave her nothing more than a grudging nod of approval and didn't stop to congratulate her.

Shocked by his rancor, even in the face of her unqualified victory, she didn't notice Dan Paulsen until he was right next to her, his gaunt face a portrait of ill will.

"Neat," he said sarcastically. "But you'll lose the appeal—you know that?"

"A hundred dollars?" she said glibly, picking up her briefcase.

But this was no game for Paulsen. It was a matter of pride and principle. "Make it a thousand," he said with poorly disguised hostility.

"Done," she told him. She would take that bet, and win.

She stepped around him and headed quickly for the door, hoping to grab Sarah. But she couldn't spot her amid all the shoving and confusion, so she followed the surging crowd out of the room and down the main corridor of the courthouse.

Outside, standing off to the side of the courthouse steps, Ben Wainwright and Jane Meyerhoff posed for the television cameras and answered the reporters' questions. Paulsen, more bitter than they over the loss, waved off the TV and newspaper journalists, and stomped away.

Katheryn also signaled the reporters that she had nothing to say to them just now. Still searching for Sarah, she peered over the heads of the people huddled on the steps. This moment needed to be shared. The victory belonged as much—if not more—to Sarah, and Katheryn needed to tell her that.

Prosecuting this case had cost her the job at Davis and Millbank, and quite possibly her position as deputy D.A. as well. Her professional future felt unclear for the first time since she had graduated from law school. But it was her finest accomplishment, and she had no regrets.

Someone called her name, and she turned around, and there was Sarah, running down the steps toward her. The grin on Sarah's face told Katheryn that she, too, had no regrets about having fought her battle for as long and as hard as it had taken to win.

A newspaper photographer caught the exact moment that they celebrated their vindication with an exuberant hug. Then they triumphantly linked arms and walked down the steps together. They had a lot to talk about.